BATLAVA LAKE

Adam Mars-Jones' first collection of stories, *Lantern Lecture*, won a Somerset Maugham Award in 1982, and he appeared on *Granta*'s Best of Young British Novelists lists in 1983 and 1993. His debut novel, *The Waters of Thirst*, was published in 1993 by Faber & Faber. It was followed by *Pilcrow* (2008) and *Cedilla* (2011), which form the first two parts of a semi-infinite novel series. His essay *Noriko Smiling* (Notting Hill Editions, 2011) is a book-length study of a classic of Japanese cinema, Yasujiro Ozu's *Late Spring*. His memoir *Kid Gloves* was published by Particular Books in 2015. His novel *Box Hill* appeared with Fitzcarraldo Editions in 2020. He writes book reviews for the *LRB* and film reviews for the *TLS*.

'No one inhabits character as intensely and subtly as Mars-Jones. *Batlava Lake* is therefore completely convincing as an everyman narrative – we know people exactly like Barry Ashton, and may even be exactly like him – but there's a larger truth here too, about clashes of cultures and history, that make this an important and highly recommended book.'
— Lee Child

Praise for *Box Hill*

'I very much enjoyed *Box Hill*. It is a characteristic Mars-Jones mixture of the shocking, the endearing, the funny and the sad, with an unforgettable narrator. The sociological detail is as ever acutely entertaining.'
— Margaret Drabble

'A tender exploration of the love that truly dare not speak its name – that between master and slave. On his eighteenth birthday, Colin literally stumbles upon a strapping biker twice his age, and falls into a long-term relationship characterised by devotion, mystery, and submission. In plain unadorned prose, Mars-Jones shows us the tender, everyday nature of this. Self-deprecating, sad, and wise.'
— Fiona McGregor

'*Box Hill* is not a novel for the prudish, but it is a masterclass in authorial control. ... Despite its diminutive length, it is rich with detail and complexity, and has plenty to demonstrate Mars-Jones's well-deserved place on any list of our best.'
— Alex Nurnberg, *Sunday Times*

'An exquisitely discomfiting tale of a submissive same-sex relationship ... perfectly realized.'
— Anthony Cummins, *Observer*

Fitzcarraldo Editions

BATLAVA LAKE

ADAM MARS-JONES

For Keith

Lake Batlava is beautiful. Deep, not exactly welcoming. I don't expect the locals think it's much like Loch Ness, but we did. I did. No legends about monsters, none that I heard of. But how would I get to hear about them anyway? I'd have to speak the language, and the Barry brain doesn't do languages. Just doesn't want to know. 'Gut und Morgen' is about as much as I can manage in foreign parts, doesn't get you far in Kosovo. Plus we weren't there as sightseers, though we saw some sights. We saw some sights.

Batlava Lake isn't just a beauty spot, civic resource into the bargain. Natural lake but improved. Enhanced. Serves as the main reservoir for a capital city, for Pristina. More than Loch Ness can say for itself, monster or not!

When I first heard the name, like everyone else did, I thought it was the same as the cakey thing. The sticky layers – Greek, is it? Likely Greek. Bit sweet for me, wherever it comes from. Baklava. When I learned the proper name I used it, Batlava, though not everybody did. They stuck with what they knew, came in handy making silly jokes. Jokes about the Baklava Lake being fed by the River Ouzo. And so on – nearly funny. Not quite.

Even if I bust a gut laughing at their jokes wouldn't make me one of the lads. They were signed-up military and I was only 'attached'. But still. I had the rank of full colonel, and they were required to salute me. Even if there were no witnesses about, the hand had to go smartly up, recognition of rank. The only snag – my hand had to stay by my side. Couldn't salute back. Wasn't allowed to.

Really knocked me off my stride first time it happened. My hand wobbled upwards of its own accord. That's how it works in films. Never a saluter who doesn't get saluted. Like when someone throws a ball at you, your hand goes up to catch it even if you weren't expecting the bloody thing to come your way, isn't that right? Your body decides and your hand goes up all by itself. How are you supposed to acknowledge a salute when you're not allowed to return it? You can't say 'Much obliged, I'm sure.' You can't say 'Thanks very much mate, appreciate it.' All you can do is behave as if nothing has happened, grow a shell. Gradually turn into the sort of plonker who expects to be acknowledged without giving anything back.

That first time I called on all my reserves, all my resistance, and went all Barry-be-strong. I sent my hand back down again, though it didn't feel right to be dropping the ball. As if I was breaking the rules, though in fact, being technical about it, I was obeying them. I noticed something, though, funny thing. There was a look in the ranker's eyes when I was starting to salute back, by that instinct I'm talking about, not being able to stop myself. You'd have to call it a smirk – at how stupid I was being. If I took the bait and showed respect for him, I was a wally plain and simple. If I played by the rules and behaved as if he wasn't there then, obviously, I was treating him like shit and I was a shit myself.

So when I managed to stop myself saluting before I was committed to the wally option, there was another look in his eyes. Different, but still pissed off. Pissed off in a new way, giving me a sort of dull glare, resentful glare. I didn't much like either of the looks that could come my way, to be honest, but there wasn't a lot I could do about it. I was trapped in the not-saluting side of things, and the lads were trapped in the saluting. None of us happy about it. After a while it seemed to me that when the ranks saluted me, their lips moved, and they mouthed a word, always the same word. I couldn't say for sure what the word was, but *squit* would be a strong candidate.

Royal Engineers don't really like being called Sappers. Fine by me. I called them Saps. If they didn't like it they still had to salute me, and I still had to not-salute back. 'Saps' are trenches. They used to have another nickname, the Mudlarks – nobody uses that one any more.

The one thing the lads couldn't deny was that, civilian or no, I was qualified. This was a fact. It was why I was there in the first place, being an 'approved person' five times over. Qualified under the Safety Rules Procedures to inspect premises and equipment and to give the go-ahead for service personnel to undertake their duties. Five tickets to my name: High Voltage/Low Voltage. Boilers & Pressure Vessels. Masts & Towers. Petrol Oil & Lubricants. Confined Spaces. They don't hand them out like sweets, those certificates. You have to study to get them, and after that you can't take your foot off the pedal, you have to refresh your knowledge every three years. Separately from your technical expertise, you have to show you can perform consistently and reliably when you're high up on a mast, or deep underground, or inside a fuel tank the size of St Paul's, whispering gallery and all – capacity of six million litres. Six *million*! No fuel in it when you inspect it, naturally, but no-one wants you inhaling those fumes, so you'll have breathing gear.

To show you can still do Confined Spaces you crawl into narrower and narrower pipes. They're real bastards with Confined Spaces. You get to do a run-through with a bit of light, without full equipment. Then it's darkness and full gear, mask, breathing apparatus, the lot. Off you go! Off you crawl. First thing you do is bump into a wall that didn't use to be there. They've changed the layout – of course they have. Breathing speeds up inside the mask. Little bit of panic. Forehead wants to sweat. Then you make yourself think, they wouldn't put me in this if there

11

was no way out. Wouldn't be allowed to! Slow down. Take your time. You don't stop being afraid but it goes away a bit and you can think round the problem. Come out of it with a bit of a grin as if you had fun.

For Masts & Towers you step off a higher gantry each time, attached to a rail with a harness – meaning your mind knows you're safe but your body never quite believes it. Your balls never quite believe it. Message doesn't reach them. No shortage of masts and towers in the Rugby area, so that's where they do it. It's not like a bungee jump. You hardly move – the harness holds you at the level you started. You have to step off into the air, that's all, but it's not everyone who can do that. It was the five tickets that had earned those salutes, not me. Not Barry as such.

The lads called me Uncle Barry, which I didn't mind. It wasn't a compliment, no, but it wasn't much of an insult either. I was comfortable with it. They all knew my track record. 'Little Uncle Barry' – not so keen on that, though I'd never claim to be the tallest. Don't often bang my head on ceilings. Little bit of an advantage in the confined spaces category. And maybe a factor in the saluting and not saluting business. More comfortable to be outranked by someone taller.

I'm not the sort to push my luck, though – always said I'd move on before anyone had the chance to call me Grandad. Not retire. I've got too much energy to retire, not now and maybe not ever. When I see people doing nothing – I don't mean workmen skiving, I mean people doing nothing in particular – I don't think, 'Get off your arses you lazy buggers,' I think, 'Where did you learn the knack of sitting still?' How did that happen? It's beyond me. If I've done the washing-up I'd rather do it again than put the things away and then find my hands are empty, no task coming up on the horizon. I like a list.

I've always had lots of energy, which came in handy as a person, five-times-approved person, with plenty on his plate. I was also married in those days, not that energy got me the approval you might be thinking in that area. Not talking about the bedroom! Carol – Mrs Barry as was, Mrs Barry Ashton – got annoyed because I would sing in the mornings. Didn't even know I was doing it. 'How can anyone wake up so bloody happy?' That was the meat of the complaint. I tried to explain that actually I don't. I don't wake up happy, I wake up cheerful. There's a difference, big difference. She couldn't seem to see it.

These days I'm always saying I'll build myself a house and find a woman who'll live in it with me, or else go at it the other way round, find a woman who wants to live with me and then build a house for the two of us – I fancy France. A woman who could handle the language side of things. Buy a dog, why not? Buy a bloody dog. Having said all that, my record with women isn't that great. Mixed, you'd have to say. I'm better with houses, though after the end of my marriage there was a woman who walked away from me with a nice house tucked under her arm. I hadn't built it but I'd certainly bought it and fixed it up, only my name wasn't on the papers. I'd trusted her, and either she saw me coming from the first or else somewhere along the line she decided to skip marriage and go straight for alimony. Her shyster was sharper than my shyster, that's what it came down to. I went with the first lawyer I found – it's not my world. How are you supposed to choose? I trusted him. Mistake. 'Fault on both sides?' I wasn't going to say that!

Mains water pressure in France is six bars. Six bars! That's enough to blow English shower fitments half way across the room – or half way across the garden if we're talking about English garden hose nozzles. I'd love to work with six bars, love to play around with that.

They called me Uncle because I was older. Also because I was there first, in the first wave of civilians. Soldiers need a place to kip, they need lights that work, toilets that flush, filters so the water's drinkable, staff for the canteen and someone to take care of payroll. People are spoiled – they think infrastructure collapse means not getting a seat on the train to work. They have no idea what the real thing is like, and neither did I, really. Not until I arrived in Pristina. So I suppose I was spoiled too. I'd done my little bit of preparation, gone out in search of a Kosovan dictionary – except there isn't one, reason being it's Albanian they speak there. Fell at the first fence! I'll take an Albanian dictionary, then, thanks. I don't do languages, never have, but give me a technical drawing or a bit of spec and I can make myself understand it, whatever language it thinks it's in. Always. Haven't tried Japanese just yet but I guarantee you I could get there in the end.

Still, a dictionary comes in handy. Keep a dictionary in your pocket and you can point at a page and hope for the best.

Everyone visiting a country for the first time will have questions to ask the military driver sent to pick them up, but maybe my questions were a bit more basic than most.

Which side of the road do they drive here? Shouldn't you choose one or the other? *No law here. Drive where you want. There's no-one to stop us. Do you see much traffic anyway?*

Where's the city? *Just coming into it. If there was electricity you'd see lights. Maybe you're here to sort that out.*

Do I smell smoke? *Affirmative. The Serbs set the sports stadium alight. It's not out yet.*

How long has it been burning? Didn't the war end last summer? *Raiding parties sneak back now and then, do a bit of damage. It'll burn for weeks yet – no-one to put it out, unless that's one of your jobs.*

Bloody hell – what was that? Why did you swerve just now? *Serbs removed all the manholes before they left. Bingo! Instant potholes. Just add boiling water – sorry, no, that's Pot Noodles. Want me to steer into the next one?*

(Little bit of a stroppy bastard. Civilian dealing with military gets used to that.)

No, you're fine. Don't listen to me. Why are we stopping? *We've arrived.*

Where's the hotel? *Just over there.*

That's the Grand Hotel? (Dark space no different from what was either side.) *Didn't I just say so? If you're in luck they'll have a generator inside.*

They did have a generator, dinky little generator – would give you a lovely old laugh if you saw it in Argos. Who's that drinking in the bar? Kate Adie. Having a tipple while the light came and went. Nice lady, and we had a friendly little chat. Quite a soft face – apple cheeks, you might say. Not what you'd expect in such a tough lady, but maybe it's a good thing, seeing she's telling people things (let's be honest) they don't really want to hear. She didn't ask me anything I wasn't allowed to answer. Official Secrets Act, she'll have caught on. When a famously fearless telly journalist, and she was hardly ever off the screen in those days, is drinking in the bar of your hotel, you don't expect too much from room service. You're lucky to have walls! A lift would have been nice but there wasn't one – well, there was a lift but it wasn't working. Tote your kit up the stairs. I was hoping for curtains, but I would have preferred windows without curtains to what I got. Curtains without windows. Curtains don't do the same job as windows, it's a fact. I slept wrapped up in everything I'd brought with me bar the passport.

15

Strictly speaking, to pick hairs, Kate Adie isn't fearless. Scared of motorbikes – won't get on one. Someone in the bar heard her saying so. Those things are dangerous.

The whole of Kosovo is some sort of funnel, sits in a ring of mountains, pulls cold air down in winter and stops it from getting out. Then come summer, the funnel fills up with unbearable heat. Kosovo is hell. Hell two ways – hellish hot, hellish cold. They used to bring jugs of water on bitter winter mornings at the 'Grand Hotel', and that's the way they were too, one day scalding hot, another freezing cold. There was never one of each! Which would have let you mix something to a human temperature so you could wash and shave to a civilized standard. By the time the scalding jug had begun to cool down I would have to get off to work. And the freezing jug, of course ... never warmed up.

There was no water in the taps. If there was, if the city had the infrastructure basics, it would be coming from Lake Batlava, of course. There's a dam and a funnel in the middle of the lake, so the overflow gets led off to supply Pristina (and Podujevo, if you're interested). Including the Grand Hotel. Where there weren't even any plugs for the basins. For a moment I thought – what, they took the manholes and the plugs too? How did they have time? Normally I'm bright in the mornings, I catch on fast, everyone says so, but I'd had a rough night. Why no plugs? Turns out it wasn't sabotage, wasn't even supply failure by the hotel. Turns out it was more of a matter of principle, Muslims being supposed to wash in running water. If you want to be impure, bring your own bloody plug! We'd had no end of briefings but nothing about a plug shortage – I might even have stayed awake for that.

We were guests in this country. That was something that was said to us, early on, more than once, and I tried to believe it. Bit of a struggle. You don't invite guests in when the house is on fire! We were something different, emergency services or clean-up crew. Or pre-clean-up crew, cleaning up before the cleaning up could start, setting up some sort of basic support system for the Royal Engineers. It was really Sappers who would be doing the dirty work, and some of it was very dirty, but they needed something in place before they could start. Which comes first, the chicken or the egg? An old riddle, but Barry here's worked out the answer. Which comes first, the chicken or the egg? What comes first is the nest. Bit of wisdom there.

Second night in the Grand Hotel I took the curtains down and wrapped myself up in them, but it was like the optician banging on at you with fiddly changes of lenses, wanting to know is *this* better or is *that* better. Can't decide. Is *this* colder or is *that* colder? Couldn't decide. They were both colder.

Our first nest was in VJ headquarters – the barracks of an army base before the Americans bombed it. We built a little camp inside the wire. Some things had been thought about and some things hadn't. Approved Persons? Present and correct, in decent numbers. There were a few of us. Competent contractors? No such luck. Hardly a one. Electricians were a special headache. They'd arrive in batches of twenty or so from Britain, flew 'em in to Skopje, bussed 'em down to us, but no screening in advance so most of them had no idea. Hopeless!

You wouldn't believe how crap they were. Get a better bunch putting cards in the Post Office saying SPARKS WANTED FOR BOOZING AND BRAWLING. SOME LIGHT DUTIES. Hopeless, just hopeless. Sort of assignment attracts piss artists. Anyone who wants to chance their arm and likes the idea of being far away from

17

home. Away from the wife and kids. They'd bring booze into the mess hall, drink themselves silly, start fights. 'Mess hall' is a bit posh for a modular prefab attached to other modular prefabs, but that was what we called it. Army lingo. Standard terms for things. You get used to it. Living conditions weren't luxurious for anybody. It wasn't the Ritz! But maybe a cut above the Grand Hotel Pristina. Windows and all sorts. Sometimes after the drinking and the fighting they'd just pass out on the floor, wake up groaning the next morning. Drag themselves off to work. Do a job pissed or hungover just as craply as the work they did stone cold sober. Or as sober as they got.

Don't talk to me about post-traumatic stress disorder. PSTD, is it? I can usually cope with abbreviations – pass me the MDF, straightforward. Make sure you read the A&ERs, fine. Common sense, them being Ammunition and Explosives Regulations. You can tell me something is ISOPfP and I'll catch on soon enough that we're talking about it being In The Spirit of Partnership for Peace. NATO lingo. Had to understand it when it was spoken to me, tried not to use it myself. But I don't deny I've got my blind spots. I have to work it out, post-traumatic stress disorder. PTSD – there it is. But with those jokers the disorder came first. There already. Stress came later, if it came at all. Some of them were weeded out and sent home, but only the worst cases, the ones who were falling apart, risk to themselves and others, and some of the ones who stayed should have joined them on that bus. Bus of disgrace.

You want to work with your hands, like me, most days you end up wading through sets of initials and piles of paperwork. In the early days of Kosovo, though, to be fair, there wasn't much pen-pushing. Pen-pushers, pro-forma jockeys, come in the second wave. After that it never stops. But early days, if there was a crucial bit of kit I was short of, I could scribble the indent on the back of an envelope and it would still happen in a hurry. That was the part I liked, making do. Making things happen on the wing. No excuses offered, none accepted.

I hated working for Essex County Council when I handled a lot of their contracts, no that's not true, liked the job, hated the shit small-minded side of it, endless rules and regs. Hated it. Can you imagine, when I went into a premises and installed or renovated a grid box – multi-gang light switch – there was strict spec about how the slots in the screw heads lined up? They had to be all vertical or all horizontal. All lined up. Nothing else would do. And we're not talking about a functional circuit, operational bit of apparatus, these were only the screws holding cover plate to base plate! And still I had to line them up for the satisfaction of some jobsworth who may never have held a screwdriver in his pasty little mitt. I had to have some arsey pen-pusher sign off on my work. Sometimes you can get a sarky thrill out of doing the work to a higher standard than what you've been asked, everything by the book and still blowing up in their faces, but this was plain brutal. No room for a come-back. I just ground my teeth. Then I thought about it and decided I'd go for north-south orientation with my screw slots. That's not something I ever thought I'd say! But if I did them east-west there was a chance some joker would come along with a spirit level. I didn't see how they were going to get up to those sorts of monkey business with north-south.

Oh, and another thing that the handbook said. Manufacturers' labels must be removed from all equipment installed. As if I had time for that! Manufacturers making sure that their name was marked on every product till the end of time, Barry scraping away to re-move the last trace of their sticky. Total waste of effort. Was it important to scratch out the makers' name on bits of kit we liked well enough to use? No. Important to make Barry feel like a berk, scrubbing away with a handful of wire wool? Seemed like it. Time to consider my options. Time to set my sights on another line of work.

There was plenty of money splashing about in Kosovo for a bit, and then outgoings got out of hand. Thirteen British bases in country altogether, costing just under £10 million apiece to build – it's for definite I saw the figure of £127 million down in black and white at one point, total outlay. But excluding running costs – those thirteen camps between them cost a few million a month to run. It was Hunting Aviation had the contract, based over in Ampthill, Lord Somebody. Lord Hunting even, maybe. Private enterprise. Don't think he made money on it! Later on he sent someone along to throw the weight around, put on the hard face, complaining about the way things were being done. Ended up making himself un-popular, till he needed an armed guard. There were plenty of people wanted him to take a thorough look around the incinerator, inspect it from close up, and they weren't shy about saying so. We'd make sure we were running it hot enough for him. Melt the bastard down for spare parts. His name? IJ – and that's all you're getting, initials. IJ, and stop right there. Go no further. There's another set of ini-tials, see – OSA. Official Secrets Act. We all signed. Even the rubbish sparks signed. I suppose – legally speaking – I'm playing with fire even talking about those rubbish sparks. I ran into a neighbour from where I used to live, Southend way, and she said, time I was first doing MOD contracts, there was someone asking about me. What was I like? Who did I drink with, who were my friends?

They'd have to check up on me, I see that, but it's a creepy old feeling just the same. Not nice. Not nice at all.

Was a time public bodies did their own maintenance, everything in-house. Value for money, common sense. Then everything changed and it was tenders and contracts, budgets and overspends, but it was still about the same thing, value for money. New kind of common sense, with everything turned upside down. Value for the taxpayer. If you were in the old system you had to adapt, get accredited, show you knew what you were about. Even when the people you were trying to impress knew a lot less than you did. Than I did. The whole system of contracting got silly, and I'm not saying I didn't benefit because I did.

This is the sort of thing that went on. HMS *Warrior*, Navy base but on land, had a new Commander. He took a look round, decided the flagpoles were shabby. Twenty-eight of them there were, one for each NATO country – flags fluttering in the breeze, lovely. But not brand spanking new. So, shall we do a refurb, smarten things up? No, reckons this Commander, we should be more long-term in our thinking. New flagpoles. Fibre glass. Never wear out – value for the taxpayer. Well, you can't buy bloody great fibre glass flagpoles in Homebase, but we bid for the contract and we managed to deliver. Proud of that. I can tell you, it was a lot easier putting up the new flagpoles than it was pulling the old ones down.

Couple of months down the line, I get a phone call from the Commander, wants a meeting. Doesn't sound happy. I go down there, ready for anything. It's like school, sometimes when you get into trouble you know why and sometimes you don't. This time I didn't know. Sometimes you cut corners – sometimes you have to. But everything was up to snuff with the flagpoles, far as I knew. And, no moving parts, there's not a lot that can go wrong!

My mistake. The halyards that hold the flag in place, they move. The flag moves, when there's movement in the air – and the air moves the whole time. Result, the lanyards crack against the flagpoles as the flag flutters to and fro, and when there are twenty-eight of them going you can't hear yourself think. You can't hear yourself plan the next bit of naval strategy or the next idea for saving public money. If they'd been a bit more long-term in their thinking they would have talked to an acoustical engineer, who would have said, well, timber flagpoles are solid and fibreglass ones are hollow, so what you'll be doing is replacing sound insulators with amplifiers. Is that really what you want?

So, the Commander says with a sigh, 'We'd better have the old ones back.' We'd better have the old ones back! As if I'd got them stacked up against the wall of my office! They'd been cut up and disposed of, long gone. Well, twenty-seven of them had. I kept one as a souvenir, and you'd not believe how hard it was to find somewhere to stow it. And that was just the one of them. So the Commander authorizes new timber flagpoles, bloody big mature trees, have to be brought from Canada, cost of a million plus. But spare a thought for the poor bloody taxpayer! He got shafted, royally shafted time after time. And I can tell you, it was a lot easier pulling the old fibre glass poles down than it was putting the new timber ones up. And maybe the fibre glass poles would have lasted for ever, but they had only a couple of months to prove it.

There will always be things that go wrong, and if you know people who can think on their feet then you should make sure you bring them with you, however the system changes. When we had the contract to maintain Chelsea Barracks there was a problem with a lift. It sounds like simple stuff – hang up an 'Out of Order' sign, get to work. It wasn't like that. There was a royal visitor, elderly, game old bird but too frail to use the stairs, and the lift had failed while she was on the upper level.

Christ! Action stations!

QM a popular lady, much more to her than waving and smiling. Little bit racy after lunch. People say gin. All I saw was Dubonnet. But this was after lunch, when the lift was kaput. In the mess people had been lined up to be introduced to her. One of them, pink angora sweater, enormous bloody cleavage, was wearing a nametag. QM says, 'I see this one is called Susan ...' looks over to the other side of the cleavage, 'What's this one called?' So, lots of fun, but just the same not someone you want to leave stranded on an upper floor during an official visit.

Lift wouldn't budge. We were frantic trying to fix it before she tottered back. Nothing doing. Praying that we'd have enough time to sort something out. Relay race of whispers, *can you keep her busy for a bit?* Well, they said, we'll try – no promises. Can't think what was said and done to slow her down, buy us a bit of time. *I wonder, Ma'am, have you looked closely at this painting? This horse just here – am I imagining things, or does it have five hooves?*

That would certainly get QM's attention. But can't work for ever. Here she comes! What's the solution? Well, QM gets into the lift at the upper level. Chap presses the button to descend, we get the signal. That's the moment we let the oil out of the hydraulics, down she comes the smooth as silk. None the wiser. Mind you, if she'd wanted to have another decko at a painting, count some more hooves, we'd have had to give her a fireman's lift to get her upstairs again.

That was part of the maintenance contract for the North London group, thirteen ceremonial sites, some you'll have heard of, some you won't. 'Ceremonial site' doesn't mean old buildings, usually does but not always. Kensington Barracks, say – Hyde Park Barracks really, but the old name sticks – that's a new building. New-ish, anyway. Household Cavalry HQ – a high-rise in Hyde Park, not what you'd expect. That wasn't a lot of fun. Too many cock-ups. Some of them I can blame on other people! Not all.

It's a small site, small footprint as they say. Hoofprint, maybe! For a cavalry barracks. Lots of demands on the building, mess facilities, lots of accommodation, which could be shoved in the tower, married quarters right at the top. The architect, whoever he was, needed to decide what happened on the ground floor. You'd think stables, but then where's the parade ground? Can't have that up in the air. So the stables ended up on the first floor, reached by a ramp. You could sometimes see horses looking out over the balcony. Always made me laugh. There were upsides and downsides, bound to be. Upside – horses can head off directly into Hyde Park, lovely thing to see. Downside – once in a while, horse loses its footing on the curved ramp. Whole atmosphere of the place changed when that happened. Terrible waste. Everyone felt sick about it.

Small site, restricted space – so small lifts. Not big enough to take the new freezers that the Prom ordered. Property Manager – Prom for short. Each property had its own budget and its own funds, not like the old days of the Property Services Administration with everything centralized. More efficient? I'm the wrong person to ask, I just get my head down and work with what's there. The new freezers were expensive bits of kit for the kitchens, double-width Fosters, but how were they going to get upstairs? In-house labour, why not? Not my idea, but it seemed to make sense. Let them earn their keep. That's the thing about telling soldiers what to do, though. You have to spell things out. Not just: take these new freezers upstairs to the kitchens. You have to say: take these new freezers upstairs to the kitchens *and don't smash them up on the way*. Wasn't said, and didn't happen. Maybe the Household Cavalry felt they were earning their keep already, defending Her Majesty and so on, not toting white goods. Get them up there! Yessir right away sir! Only they're useless when they get there, have to be chucked out and re-ordered, with a few angry memos bouncing around the building saying don't let that happen again.

Where I came unstuck was similar, or different, depending how you think. I was told, 'Clear out the old electrical equipment' from the building. Up the top of the building, above married quarters, the nerve centre if you like. That was what I was told, and that was the message I passed on. Clear out the old electrical equipment. Yessir right away sir! Out it all went, the old electrical equipment, including the radio equipment that made it possible to have proper communications, keep tabs on activity round the Palace. Advantage of a high-rise building, you get a radio mast that you don't have to put up. So the question is, are radios electrical? And I'd say yes. If you want radio equipment left in place, you say, clear out the old electrical equipment but leave the radio stuff strictly alone. It's electrical but we want it to stay. Yessir right away sir! Old electrical equipment gets chucked out, radio equipment stays where it is.

So for a few days Close Protection didn't have proper comms, had to use walkie-talkies, radio waves being line-of-sight and the tower of Hyde Park Barracks not seeing anything much at the moment. Bit of a blow to their pride but no harm done long term, though it was a good while

25

before I was bought a drink in that particular mess. So maintenance always has a stressful side, comes with the territory. You just hope nobody notices what nearly went wrong, and when it really goes wrong you hope the press doesn't get hold of it. Kosovo was more of the same, only with no royals. No royals and no rules. There was stress from day one. Stress came with that territory, without a doubt. Can't deny it. Traumatic stress? Maybe that too, couldn't say. Never saw a doctor, never spoke to one. On top of the regular stress, which there had to be, stands to reason, arriving in a strange country and starting from scratch, trying to rebuild it from the ground up. From a standing start, everything in ruins. Case in point, here's a for-instance – we were having trouble with an electricity substation in the middle of nowhere. Not quite the middle of nowhere, as it goes, more the edge of nowhere. That's where you put a substation, to drop the voltage. It can go fast as you like cross country but it needs to slow down when it gets near a town, safety protocols.

In this substation, one I'm talking about, the system had blown and not reset automatically. Now, different countries have different ways of building substations. Everybody's different. What the Jugoslavs did, back when that's what they were, Jugoslavs, and they were building things and not smashing them up, was put up these tidy little blockhouse affairs. When we went into this one, we could smell something before we could see anything. Not a strong smell, not a stench, and not completely horrible. Something nice in it somewhere. Barbecue. The poor bastard who had been sheltering there had got himself too close to the buzz bars – copper tubes held by ceramic fixtures they were, going up the wall like rungs of a ladder. He climbed that ladder all right. Took all those rungs in a leap. He was scraps of old burned meat on bones,

26

with some charred rags keeping a few bits of him out of sight. What was left was curled up against the bottom bars, that being why the current had been interrupted. If he'd fallen clear then the system would have reset. I doubt if he'd gone mad and run at the bars though who's to say. More likely he'd just got too close. It was a confined space, after all. Spark across the gap and that was that. Frying tonight. He'd come in from the cold and got warm all right. I wonder how long he'd been there before it happened. No food, no water. Nothing to keep a person alive. The blockhouse had a couple of small windows – no curtains – it had even less going for it than the Grand Hotel in Pristina. Wasn't our job to collect the body, just get the current back on. Corpse Retrieval not one of my tickets, thanks very much. Somebody else's headache to work out where he should end up. Finding the people, whoever they were, who would need to know.

I didn't mind my little modular billet at VJHQ, technically for two though I never had to share. Snug, as a bug, in a rug, thanks. Toasty warm. I like the bottom bunk. Everything was modular, built up from little boxes, two-man billets, whether it was a 25-man camp or battalion strength, five hundred men. I saw modules in my dreams. Corridor down the middle, ablution block at the end. I didn't have en-suite, of course, but if walking to the ablution block counts as hardship then I'm hard as you like. Perk of the job, not sharing quarters, like a tax code beginning NT – Not Taxable. Lovely! My all-time favourite set of initials, fave rave and top of the pops, plain unforgettable.

Some people want to fix things, some just sit around waiting for someone else to do it. I always needed to do something with my hands, even if it was only taking things apart to put them back together. My Dad was pretty handy himself, plus he knew when something was beyond him and how to find someone with that little extra bit of skill or savvy. When I was quite a little kid, six maybe, we drove to Italy, yes drove to Italy, to visit Dad's brother's grave. My Uncle Paul. A kid that age doesn't ask, Dad, why are we going so far? What's going on, really? Why isn't Mum coming? Child that age, kiddy of six, has just the one question. Asks, Can I bring my toys?

I remember the wooden cross on his grave, and the big hole in the wall behind it. At the time I thought he'd actually died where they'd buried him, the wall all damaged by bullets or bits of a bomb, and I wondered why they didn't patch it up. I already said I was six! That trip was the only time I remember us being alone together.

They put up a memorial to the first British soldier killed in Kosovo while I was there. Not killed in action, mind – turned his Land Rover over. Casualty of war just the same. I've driven on those roads. We paid a visit there once, me and a few of the lads. Just a stone pillar with a ring of grass round it and some fencing – all looking a bit tatty. So we cleaned the stone up, strimmed the grass, painted the fencing. Little enough to do for the bloke.

Then on the return journey from seeing Uncle Paul's grave a stone hit the windscreen of our Morris Eight. Cracked it right across. Dad asked around – well, he waved his hands at the windscreen and threw them out wide, then saw where people pointed their fingers – and he found someone who could make us a new one. That's right – make a new one. This mechanic he found, handyman, whatever he was, spent a long time taking measurements, marking up a new piece of glass. Then he laid a wire in exactly the right position. Measured again. Checked. Didn't hurry about getting everything exactly so. When he was satisfied everything was exactly right he connected the wire to a car battery. The wire glowed red, then white, and the man dashed a pail of water over it. The glass cracked off round the wire, and then all he had to do was tidy up, smooth the edges. Magic! New car windscreen, homemade with no fuss. Of course you can only do the trick with a flat windscreen, but that's how they were in those days, flat. I was probably already in love with making things work, with making things do what they're supposed to, but afterwards it was for definite. It was all set up, properly fixed in place, what I wanted to do with my days.

There were things about Italy I didn't like. I didn't like strange ladies coming over and making a fuss of me, lifting me onto their laps and cooing. Pawing me. I learned to run and hide when they made their move. They couldn't even get my name right – called me Bambi. Bambi! I ask you.

I didn't like the food in Italy, told Dad it was 'too tasty'. Only natural. Everything was different, nothing was the same – breakfast wasn't corn flakes. Tea wasn't beans on toast. Maybe Dad was trying to decide whether to stay in a rotten marriage just for my benefit. Only thought about that afterwards, of course. Normally I do well on tests – but I must have failed that one, didn't I?

I made my own trip to Uncle Paul's grave after my marriage broke up. Solo trip. You can rely on dead people, they stay put! They don't decide things aren't perfect and move on. The cemetery wall still hadn't been mended but there was a reason for that, good reason. It wasn't just a wall in Rome, it was a Roman wall! So it wasn't broken, it was just old. The great big holes – they were part of it. The wooden cross had gone, and there was a proper stone one. I doubt if Dad paid for that! And the other thing that had changed was the trees. They'd been busy, the trees.

First time I saw them they were saplings, not much more than my height, but now they were looking down at me from forty feet above.

A lot of the time in early Kosovo days we civilians had more to do than the Saps did. When the ground is frozen and you can't dig foundations, can't bury generators, simple things get to be bloody difficult. The power station was fired up with lignite. What's lignite? Glad you asked. Lignite is shit, that's what lignite is. Lignite is coal that needs another few million years to ripen up, be worth burning. Filthy stuff. Snow goes brown all around when you burn it. Plus the locals dig it up from just under the surface. Then they're surprised their houses fall down. Sometimes you have to despair of people, just give up hope. When people won't be helped.

If it didn't snow then it was almost worse, with a foot of fog hugging the ground that must be the coldest thing in the world. One poor Sap wearing Doc Martens, not the newest pair, found he could hardly move his feet after they sucked up water into the little cell compartments in the soles and then froze solid.

Not much to entertain the military while we struggled to set things up, and the military were bored. Bored out of their tinies. Some of our lot went a bit mad doing up their bases. The Yanks set the standard. They had to do everything on a larger scale. Of course they did! Their bases had McDonaldses, bowling alleys, the works. A hundred flavours of ice cream while the locals had no heating.

We at BritFor didn't go in for anything elaborate. Over at Waterloo Lines they put a lot of effort into building a bar that was colossal. It was as long as a bus, even a bus and a half, and some of the lads there got it into their heads to decorate the top of it. So what they did was take

30

pfennigs and superglue them to the top of the bar, which was deep as well as long. They must have used, what, a couple of hundred thousand pfennigs? Deutschmarks being the local currency, not officially, but good luck doing business in dinars. So they created a shortage of pfennig coins – only destabilized the local economy! That wasn't the plan. It was just a side effect, distraction that got well out of hand.

After they had finished they poured resin over the bar top and I have to say it looked spectacular. They let the chogies fight over it when they left. Who probably found a way of melting the resin, though it's not a job I'd like to be landed with on that scale. Not with your mates jostling you for their turn with the blowtorch – jostling or wrestling but certainly not waiting their turn.

I probably shouldn't call them chogies but I'm not being rude. There wasn't any bad feeling against them – as there was with some of our supposed colleagues, of other nationalities. The French were in charge of making sure WFA was put in the fuel supply (winter fuel additive, or even plain anti-freeze) but there were always murmurings that the fucking Frogs, pardon my ... well I have to say French, don't I?, had forgotten to do it or had nicked the stuff and sold it on.

Some of our lads said the chogie women were whiffy, which was true but I told the lads straight out they were whiffy too, who didn't have excuses when it came to washing facilities. You know where the ablution block is, off you go – don't forget behind your ears and behind your balls. We had to watch the chogie ladies, mind, but that's standard. They would strip the canteen if you didn't watch them like hawks. I'm not talking about pilfering. Blind eyes can be turned to a little of that. One look at their faces and you know they're not exactly profiteering.

I'd only get involved when I saw one who'd made a sort of kangaroo pouch under her apron out of a sheet of plastic. Tipping whole bowls of food into it. Do it on the quiet and you might get away with a certain amount – but don't take the piss.

You had to watch the men as well but their little ways were different. They knew that tools were checked in and out on a daily basis, and no-one went home (wherever their homes were) until everything was accounted for. So they wouldn't be able to half-inch a screwdriver – but an electric drill? Different matter. They would take the drill out of the case, the drill and all the bits. Replace them with stones. That way it wouldn't feel light when it was checked back in. Next day when we find the stones it's too late to identify the guilty party. The chogies all just shrug, though it's more of a what-do-you-expect? kind of shrug than an I-didn't-do-it. That kind of shrug. And our lads don't really believe all chogies look alike, but they're not going to be able to pin it on any one of them. So we're going to be checking every box from now on, adding an extra fifteen minutes of faff to our day, so thanks for that. Thanks a lot.

The drills would turn up in the markets in Pristina. Not a lot of use, you'd think, in a city without electricity, but you could buy a generator at the same time and then you'd be in business. It may have been crime, but at least it was organised, in a country where nothing else was. You could even buy a brand new BMW. You could buy a fleet, come to that – they must have nicked a transporter. God knows where they got a transporter-load of BMWs from, but it can't have been Kosovo. So you could drive around in a BMW without paying an arm and a leg, as long as you didn't mind feeling your tyres sink into melting tarmac in summer, or driving in the ice-ruts left by previous traffic in winter. And of course you could never take it out of the country unless you were in a mood to be arrested.

As a civilian I've always tried to build a team, to keep things running smoothly, and I understand military morale is a different animal. Moody animal. Surly animal. Boredom and insecurity don't mix, or maybe they do. Turn into something else. How are you going to feel secure in a country where it's drummed into you that *if you didn't bloody drop it, don't bloody pick it up* ...? You're told to treat every cigarette packet as a booby trap, not a piece of litter. If it's litter no harm done, but pick up something that's wired to explode ... and you won't have time to wish you had listened.

I bodged up a coat rack for the mess, just stuck a metal rod into a mine the Serbs had left behind. Nobody really noticed till they had Mine Awareness training, then everyone got jitters. As if I'd leave the primer charge in! I'm not stupid.

It wasn't easy to keep in touch with spouses, families. Spouses is the official word. There were mobile phones around in the UK, no coverage in Kosovo, naturally. To phone home you had to make an appointment, be given a time slot. Easier to keep in touch by post, if you've got the gift of putting things on paper. All very old-fashioned really, throwback to BFPOs for writing to our boys in uniform, *Two-Way Family Favourites* at twelve noon on a Sunday – though of course 'in Germany it's one o'clock'.

If something came for you in the post, you'd get a slip, chitty, saying we have something for you to collect at your earliest convenience. One time I got a chitty, went and signed for my parcel, just about to take it away when they said, do you mind opening it, sir?

Why's that? Think it's contraband? No real reason, sir, it's just that it bleats every time we move it. Goes *baa*.

Every time. Must be a reason.

So I had to open the package with everyone looking, and yes, it bleated every time anyone moved it. I had a sort of inkling even before the wrapping was off. The girls at Brize Norton liked me – I'd been pretty much in charge of Brize Norton, not meaning rank but meaning running the place day to day. Only the largest station the RAF has, so plenty to keep me busy. And the girls knew I was going somewhere cold. So they'd knitted me a willy warmer – sock, really, but meant for somewhere else, no question. They'd fitted it with a little device that made a bleating sound every time it moved. You get them in greetings cards, those little chips – sure you've seen them. Give your old Granny a heart attack when she opens her birthday card.

Somebody must have told the girls at Brize Norton there were lots of sheep in Kosovo. Maybe it's even true, can't say I saw a lot in that line. Maybe they were think- ing of the Falklands? Or – simplest explanation – there wasn't a lot on offer in the novelty shop! The sound of wild dogs howling would have been a better fit for Kosovo, in the way of being more true to life. Not so much of a joke, though.

To speak to Carol I'd book a time and make the call from a cramped little cabin, not even soundproof. I hate writing letters. Hate it. Real struggle to get to the foot of the page, then if I make it all the way down there I'll sign off right away, not go through the grief of anoth- er page. Even if the bottom bit gets a bit squashed up. Carol was always complaining about my letters. *Why do you find it so hard to tell the boys you love them?* I don't. It's not hard, I'm always saying it. *You put 'Regards'!* No, look, see there – 'Regards from your loving Dad.' Squashed up a bit, maybe. Definitely there. I mean, what more am

I supposed to do? Everybody's different. That's me. We can't all be the same.

I was on the wrong side of forty when I got hitched, and maybe I was a catch and maybe I wasn't. But I was what Carol wanted at the time. I wasn't some kid with a sports car. Maybe she thought I was a pushover, and most of the time I was.

I did have a sports car, matter of fact – just not the sort that gets the girls going, because they only know a few names, from films. Ooh Aston Martin, ooh Ferrari, ooh E-type Jag! AC Cobra, what's that? It wasn't sleek and shiny, I can tell you that, bit tatty but mechanically sound. Lovely thing to drive. Aluminium body, so fantastic power-to-weight. Right-hand drive but I didn't mind that.

One night, parked outside our first house, it was set alight and burned away to ... well, nothing. Close to nothing. That's how it is with aluminium. Maybe I should have put it in a garage, but that's just hindsight talking. It wasn't a condition of the insurance. It's just that the petrol cap didn't come fitted with a lock. More trusting age and so on – anyone with a match could have made it happen. Don't think I can pin it on Carol!

Then the war started with the insurers. They wouldn't cough up. Technicality – I'd reconstructed some of the paperwork, to save them time, which they said invalidated the claim. Why? Legal owner, insurance in place. Pay up! Nothing yet, but I can wait. Forget it, Barry, people say, it's ancient history. Haven't you heard of the statute of limitations? But that's criminal law, isn't it? This is civil, and I have an active claim. My claim is active, file's ready to go. The day I turn on Radio 2 and hear that reconstructed documents have been accepted in an insurance claim – just one – then I'm back in business. And the moral is, hang on to paperwork. Every scrap!

Bride and groom aren't supposed to see each other on their wedding day before the big moment, but that didn't stop Carol showing up at mine on our wedding morning before she got dressed, to make sure I was up to snuff. Kit inspection! That's what it was like. She'd brought along her own choice of tie, as if I was a little boy who couldn't look after himself. I had my own tie, thank you very much. Put those two ties next to each other and I swear you couldn't tell them apart. Dark blue jobbies both of them, tasteful, little bit of a stripe. But she had to put her one round my neck just to be sure. Tied it on me herself – must have been taking lessons! Big fat knot. Practising on her old Dad, or maybe borrowed a dummy from the Sue Ryder. Wouldn't put it past her. Borrowed, not bought or stolen, because she was working at the Sue Ryder at the time, couple of hours most mornings. Then she ruffled my hair, yes I had hair, and said she'd see me in church. Nothing to stop me changing back to my own tie, so that's what I did. Point of honour. I'm not a kid!

And I suppose the ties weren't i-dent-i-cal after all, because she spotted the swap at once. Fumed all the way through the service. Sighed and rolled her eyes so much I didn't think she'd be able to come out with 'I do' before she started on the bollocking that was due to me. You can see it in the wedding photographs. Let's just say she has high colour. It was touch and go whether the wedding night would be a joyride or a whole night's worth of nagging, and-another-thing, and-another-thing. Bit of both as it turned out.

I'm not good on the phone, I'm not good on paper, I can't always put things into words even face to face. So what am I good for? I'm good around the house. Even Carol always said so. Like to tidy up, get things orderly, enjoy fixing things, rehang a door without mentioning it. It gave me a kick watching her expression when she knew something had been changed for the better, and she couldn't quite work out how or what. The freezer door not bashing into anything, case in point. She'd been going on at me about it, and then it was all fixed but I told her I hadn't done anything. You must be imagining things, Carol, I said – it's always been hinged that side. This is the way it's always been. Don't you remember, darling? Want me to change it back, my love? Except I shouldn't have said that, giving the game away, back to square one. No good at playing games, no good at lying, rubbish husband material altogether.

I've heard blokes on the phone to wives or girlfriends swear black is white and get away with it. Go all the way from *whose-knickers-are-those?* to *how-could-I-ever-have-doubted-you-darling?* Talk themselves all the way from doghouse to bedroom – to the warmest part of the bed! Then they hang up and go back to the bit on the side and catch my eye, as in *what are you looking at?* Nothing. I can't explain. I can't begin to do it. Not in me. Should ask for lessons, really, but don't want to learn. It's a case of does exactly what it says on the tin. You know what you're getting. That should be enough.

If you're not good on paper and hate talking on the phone then being bollocked on the phone by your missus for not writing good enough letters to your kids has to be as bad as it gets. She'd say, *Barry, have you written to Kevin about that book you're both supposed to be reading? Because he struggles with his reading at the best of times, which maybe you don't remember on account of not going to parents' evenings more than once in a blue moon.*

It's true we'd made an agreement to read a chapter a week of *Stig of the Dump*, shaken hands on it and everything, only apparently I wasn't keeping my side of the bargain. *He's only reading it to please you, you know – all his friends are reading about wizards. He's the only one stuck with a caveman.* I didn't know what to say. What was the complaint, exactly? I wasn't keeping up with my home-work, or the pair of us were reading the wrong bloody story? He chose it! Maybe before wizards got so popular. I couldn't do right for doing wrong, and nothing was ever good enough in her book.

I buckled down and read *Stig of the Dump*, in my bunk at night, not wanting the lads to know I was reading a kiddies' book. I wrote the letters as instructed, and I don't expect they were any good but that's a different matter. I fulfilled my contract, which is what I do. I tell a lie, there was a bit at the end of the book that gave me a little bit of a surprise, nice surprise. The boy in the book can't sleep one night and ends up time-travelling back to Stig's time, don't ask me how, Stig being an actual throwback from the past, and helps his tribe finish off building Stonehenge! If not Stonehenge then something like it. So I wrote to Kevin saying, *it's a mystery how they moved those stones, son. We still don't know. No-one knows.* But really it was Carol I wanted to sit up and take notice. *Stig's not a caveman, you twit, he's an engineer! Stig's tribe is my tribe too.* Put that in your pipe and smoke it.

Carol wanted me to talk about my feelings, but she flipping hated it when I did. What she wanted was for me to feel the same as her. Different thing. Funny thing was, Carol liked to have me under her thumb, but you'd have to say the times the sparks really flew, sex-wise, was when I'd reached my limit and told her what was what. Times when anything-for-a-quiet-life wasn't even an op-tion. There were some nights, after a real slanging match, when we could hardly wait to get the kids to bed. I'd be in the shed, but really I was just tinkering, and when Carol shouted out, 'Are you going to be in there all bloody night, Barry?' I'd know we were on. Korma is always tasty, nothing wrong with a nice creamy korma, but sometimes – you just feel like vindaloo. Tell me I'm wrong! Burnt tongue and not minding. She had nothing to complain about in the bedroom department, and I have to say she knew what she was about. Hearty appetite. Afterwards she'd call me Tiger and I'd call her Beetroot from the way she looked in those wedding photographs, till I twigged she didn't like being reminded. It wasn't supposed to be mentioned, had to go into Room 101. Gone for good, binned. Never happened.

People say you need shared interests to make a relationship last. I wouldn't know! Never found a woman who spoke my language, so you have to get by, don't you, bodging it, same as with any job that isn't hundred per cent up to code. Can't be too precious about fit and finish. I didn't mind watching TV shows that were her cup of tea and not mine, though I didn't always keep my lip zipped. *Brookside*, for instance, when the papers could be full of someone's body buried under a patio. Lead item! But it was only on telly and not real at all. I wouldn't mind if Carol had been a fan, but she only started watching when the murder stuff was in the papers. She said she wanted to find out what all the fuss was about! I couldn't see the point. But to each his own. And – other side of the coin – she never slept as soundly as she did on the sofa next to me during *Top Gear*. Before Jeremy Clarkson had been thought of ... well, before he joined the programme, anyway. Little lady snores, she made. I tape-recorded her doing it once. Which she didn't appreciate!

Kosovo was always a problem between us, though I couldn't work out why. She knew my line of work, knew I had to commit to a long stretch or not bother at all. It's living overseas, sorting a country out, not nipping to Calais on a booze cruise. She didn't seem to understand that if you're a contractor you sign a contract! And that's it. Legally binding. Though it's also true, once you're there you lose touch with the life back home. Sometimes I'd forget to arrange a phone call, and other times I'd arrange a call and then forget. I'm not making excuses, but I had enough to keep straight without worrying about kids' homework, or making a phone call that's ninety per cent chivvying and only a little bit of the stuff that fills my tank, cheerful chat, news of the boys or lovey talk.

I enjoyed the sweet talk, lovey talk, pillow talk, but couldn't join in. Just not in me. Plus I was in a ramshackle office while she was tucked up comfy on the sofa, if not actually in bed. And then after a while Carol got bored with making all the running, and I can't really blame her for that. Then the chivvying was closer to a hundred per cent, and who wants that?

I tried to talk to her about what I was seeing. *The people here have nothing. Nothing. And they're the lucky ones – the ones who have nothing.* She heard something different from what I was saying. She thought I was rubbishing her life and everything in it. I wanted her to enjoy the kids, the house, everything. I wasn't rubbing her nose in things. What I was trying to say was, *We have everything, everything we need and bit left over. Can't we stop fighting about things that don't matter?*

Some of the Saps heard there was a restaurant opening in town. It didn't seem likely, with all the problems with food supply, but a party of us went along to see what it was like. It turned out be an old car showroom, and either the plate glass had survived by some miracle or more likely been replaced. Either way it had been painted black, so from outside you couldn't see a thing. Someone was tackling little refurbishment projects – or not so little. Rival infrastructure building, if you want to look at it that way.

When we went inside I could feel our lads bristle, and they more or less formed a circle round me and Rodge, the only other civilian in our party, auxiliary, support-staff, whatever you want to call us. Rodge is a big boy, but I don't think he minded having the lads' protection. Yes, I know, when they circle the wagons in a Western it's the women and children get put in the middle when there are redskins about. Redskins, Native Americans, whatever. There was a sinister feel about the place. There were tables and chairs but no place settings and no cutlery. No smell of cooking either, just rough tobacco. We sat down just the same, and waited for someone to come over to us. He wasn't much like a waiter.

We ordered drinks, and he seemed to understand although he didn't write anything down. Some old-fashioned waiters are like that, don't make a note of anything and never make a mistake – point of pride. He turned away and we called him back, and someone said we wanted some grub and called him mate. Not aggressive but could have sounded that way. 'Steaks all round, okay, matey?' Bit of an edge, maybe.

There was some chat while we waited for drinks. One of the ranks, name of Micky, was talking about his wedding plans. Stag in Prague, hen in Barcelona, wedding reception for two hundred in Leighton Buzzard, honeymoon in Dubai. What? Why? What's going on? They were planning two years ahead. They'd have to, operation on that scale. I know about infrastructure, and I wouldn't tender for the job. Rather rebuild a broken country any day than face a bridesmaid who doesn't fancy the colour of her dress, thinks it doesn't suit her complexion! I said to Micky, 'What's your hurry to see the world? Don't you want to keep something back for your golden wedding? That's what you want to do, mate.'

Micky didn't take to that. 'Don't start with the you-don't-want-to-do-it-like-that routine, Barry,' he said. 'It's only funny on the telly.' I didn't follow. Wasn't going to ask what he meant and risk looking a fool – you have to keep your end up with the lads.

Then a young Sap, proper baby squaddie, baby face but blue chin from a strong growth, asked me if I'd had weapons training. Hand of friendship, maybe? Maybe he'd had a bellyful of the wedding saga and wanted to cheer me up after the brushing-off I got from Micky. Or trying to make an opening, crack the Barry case. Or else, trying to find someone even more useless than him! It took me aback and I was a bit short with him. I said no, which was a bit of a dodge. I mean, I have and I haven't. I'm not saying it never happens that one of the military expresses an interest, personal interest, but ... it never happens!

Drinks arrived, but they weren't what we ordered. Not beer but the local stuff. Someone sniffed it and said, 'What's this muck?'

'Is rakia.'

'We want beer. Beer is what we drink.'

'Is rakia.' He went away.

We decided we would drink the rakia while we were waiting for our beers. After that we would drink our beers while we waited for our steaks. I don't know what rakia does for chogies but it certainly slowed our thinking down. When they brought more rakia Rodge said, 'What's happened to our steaks?' Then he said, 'Did we ask for them to be well done? We should say they need to be well done. Can't stand them fucking pink.' By now I was wondering what we had got ourselves into. I tried to tell him that no steaks were coming. Not well done, not medium, not rare. If we didn't play our cards right, steak knives were what we might be seeing before too long. That was my line of thought. Getting anxious. Still, Rodge wasn't going to risk missing out on a feed by backing down. He told the waiter that he had five minutes to produce our steaks. I say waiter, but if he had ever looked like a waiter he didn't any more. This wasn't someone who earned a living bringing people what they want. Rodge raised his hand with the fingers spread, to spell out the number five, and said, very no-nonsense, '*Mate – well done.*' That's normally quite a nice thing to hear – well done, mate!, you got double top or whatever – but my heart sank. Rodge's 'mate' had a real edge on it now. In his head maybe he was in the pub back home and about to cut up rough. For no real reason. And I know there are parts of the world where raising your hand like that puts the evil eye on people. I was hoping Kosovo wasn't one of them.

The words worked like a magic spell on the waiters, though not in a good way. Bad magic. Bad juju. Hard to believe we had ever thought of them as waiters. What's the word? Service staff. Suddenly there were five of them between us and the door. They can't have had more gold teeth between them than they did a few seconds earlier. Maybe we could just see them more clearly now, the gold teeth. New idea: if there was nothing to stop us doing what we liked here then there was nothing to stop other people, people like this, doing what they liked either. Maybe Kosovo was like a burning building and some of the people there had called the fire brigade, but other people didn't want the flames put out. Might have set the fires themselves.

There was a smell in the air. Maybe it was danger and

maybe it was steroid pong, in which case, well, it could have been either side giving off the aroma. Some of our lads were big, swollen to bursting almost.

I said, 'Let's pay and go, shall we?', nice and quiet. Rodge said, quite loud, 'We're not paying.' I didn't think the *rakia* was all that bad, though it's true we hadn't ordered it. There are some civilians, like Rodge, who automatically feel safe around the armed forces, and then there are the ones who can almost hear scary words spoken on the radio. '... *one of several auxiliary personnel caught in a crossfire* ...' That's more me. Uncle Barry wanted to go home.

It was proper slow-motion deadlock, like a film, with everybody hauling up aggression from low down in their guts, until Rodge picked up a chair. I thought, what's the idea, Rodge? Where are you going with this? Then he threw it against the wall – the wall that was really only a window. That's where he was going with it. The wall shattered and went away. Also like a film. Suddenly we could see even more of the gold teeth, because their mouths were hanging open just as wide as ours were. Everyone but Rodge in his moment of inspiration had forgotten they weren't really walls, just painted glass, and it took a moment to put the world back together from the bits of it crashing down. Then we legged it. Normally I like to think things through, make a list of options, but there was nothing normal about the set-up. Looking before you leap definitely off the menu. Speaking for myself, I'm not going to break a window off my own bat, but if there's a window broken I'm not going to gawp at the view for more than a second – I'll shift over to the side of it where the gangsters aren't. Up and over! Good job there wasn't an open manhole waiting for me there. Out of the frying pan and into the manhole.

Then we were round the corner and panting with re-lief and excitement – all of us panting, I can keep up the pace on a short spurt. Rodge was shouting, 'Monster! *Monster!* Did you see that? See what I did!' Safe assump-tion. 'Knocked the wall down! Broke the fucking window like a fucker!' He and Micky were high-fiving each other, but I hung back. I know – a salute I could have been in on, and I missed it! Only realized after. But I needed to get my breath back though that wasn't the whole story. My hands had found a place for themselves after the sprint, shield-ing my balls. They had to stay there for a bit. The lads giggling like naughty schoolboys when we'd been lucky, not clever. Not clever at all. I was thinking how different-ly it could have played out. Bodies and headlines. Sordid brawl, casualties. Who wants to go like that?

Reason it was a dodge about weapons training is this. No training for combat or anything like, but plenty of ex-perience with shooting as a skill and a hobby. Hate the word, though – I mean hobby, not skill. If you've concen-trated on something and spent a lot of time exploring it, then hobby is the wrong word, insulting word.

I got a lot out of rail shooting. Very satisfying activity. Shooting of great precision from a gun fixed in place, with no stock, at very long range. I did well with 1500 metres. The gun is just a barrel, with a receiver where the rounds go in. You manufacture your own rounds, or at least I did. A mighty satisfaction for an engineer, to turn up your own projectiles. I made my own tracers to add to the fun. I used to shoot at Bisley, at the place the National Rifle Association has there. Yes, there's a British NRA, older than the American one. No, Charlton Heston had no connection with it, none.

You've machined your ammunition to the highest degree of precision, so if your grouping on the target is loose and you want to blame the manufacturer just look in a mirror. Now it's your job to calculate the trajectory of each round to the same standard. Anything and everything can affect the way a projectile behaves. Temperature, wind speed, air density – the vectors are always shifting, with every air current, thermal or moment of turbulence having a knock-on effect. Everything changing from one minute to the next. If you get the calculation wrong there's no excuse – the mechanism had a faulty part, and the faulty part was you. When your grouping is so tight on the target *it's like the pads on a kitten's paws* ... something I heard said in the clubhouse at Bisley. Posho voice but not a total idiot if he could say something like that. You want your shots as tightly grouped on the card as the pads on a kitten's paws. That's exactly the feeling, thrill of a tight cluster. And when it happens and everything has gone just as well as it possibly could then just for a moment. For a moment you might wish there was someone to share your moment of triumph with, but it'd take so much explaining that even if a mate showed up with a big smile and a couple of beers you'd wish he wasn't there a moment later.

When I mention rail shooting some people don't know what I'm talking about, and I have to explain about the NRA and no Charlton Heston. There have been also been one or two who've said, 'Oh, you mean bench-rest shooting?' More formal description. And they're the ones who *think* they know what they're talking about, and they assume you should be competing if you do it at all, taking part in team events and so on. I just don't see the point of all that. Competing against yourself is always the real sport, isn't it? If you want a social club, join one. If you like doing something on your own, don't drag other people into it.

It's a gentlemanly sort of sport in its hi-tech way, so of course brutally simple weapons, like automatics and even semi-automatics, are completely against the rules. But what stops a gun like a Galil assault rifle – lovely weapon, Israeli – from firing all twenty-five rounds in its magazine one after the other, without your hand leaving the trigger? I was thinking about that one day at Bisley. A little catch, that's what, a little catch called the cere. I don't know if that's even the right way of spelling it. The sear? I expect it's the cere. So I filed away the cere, just to see if that was really all there was to it. My feeling was that the gas pressure would return the chamber, and without the cere to hold it back the next round would load and fire all by itself. You know the *THRRRRRRRRP* noise guns make in action films? Well, that's the sound that was suddenly echoing across the grounds of NRA Bisley. Bingo – automatic fire. And it's amazing how the barrel climbs in those circumstances. Went right up into the sky. Suddenly the gun had a mind of its own. If I'd done it more than once I might have learned to correct for that, but that was me done. I put away my Galil, my modified Galil, and never fired it again. Because of what it was. My illegally modified Galil, currently what they're always looking for when there's a scandal in the newspapers. Smoking gun, in so many words! My engineer's what-if had turned into something else in no time flat. Criminal enterprise. Luckily there's an army firing range backing onto Bisley. With luck anyone who heard a dodgy noise would think they'd made a mistake and it was coming from the other direction.

I don't get bored easily, I get swallowed up by what needs doing. I'm good at screening out the side issues, things that may be important but don't have to be dealt with *right now*. One thing at a time and it all gets done.

Even so, I was restless, wanted an excuse to go off base without getting into the usual sorts of trouble. Booze and women.

I decided to do some bird-watching – always loved birdsong, couldn't tell you why, and often it's the smaller birds that have the richest song. Making no claim for myself! I had decent binoculars, and I fancied seeing a pygmy cormorant on Lake Batlava, though it's probably not even the right habitat, and a pygmy cormorant isn't exactly a songbird. I'd not even seen a picture, but it stood to reason that the pygmy cormorant got to be called that way from looking like a cormorant, only not so big. After a while keeping still with my binoculars, I started to feel very exposed. I could see the funnel and the dam that feeds it with the overflow. That was intact. But there must have been a walkway leading out there, and the Serbs had smashed most of it. You could see where it had been, from traces of wreckage. Masonry just breaking the surface. Had to be the Serbs, on their way out. Smashing everything they could. I wondered if maybe they'd not had the time to wreck the funnel, make a proper job of it. With a bit more trouble they could have made even more work for people like me – seemed to be their priority.

There's nothing like looking through binocs in a half-destroyed country to make you feel you're in the crosshairs yourself. Bloody big target painted on the back of your head. At that time I didn't even know bird-watchers, proper bird-watchers, were called twitchers, but I could have come up with the name myself. I felt twitchy just lying there, and after a minute or two my scalp was crawling and I couldn't wait to stop. No pygmy cormorant for me that day. I know serious birdspotters would have a good giggle seeing me on my belly for ten minutes and expecting to see something special.

Boredom gets soldiers into trouble, and nervy boredom is the worst kind. So if I was beginning to get restless, like I said, then the lads were proper bored. Bored out of their tinies. A peace-keeping mission isn't supposed to be exciting, I know that – boredom means it's working. Try telling that to the lads! Not many of us, military or civilian attached, are any good at sitting still. I know I'm not. Rather do something than nothing. So I wrote a letter to Carters Seeds asking if by any chance they had old stock they could send us, stuff past its sell-by date that we could just bung in the ground and get some growth going, hoping to cheer everyone up, chogies and peace-keeping forces alike. I didn't hear anything back, and I'd started to get used to the idea that they were all thorough-going unpatriotic wankers at Carters Seeds. Then I was told there was a package waiting for me. Two packages, actually, and anyway 'package' didn't give any idea of the size of the things. There were several hundredweight of seeds, and you get a hell of a lot of seeds to the pound. To the ounce, even. I should have realized that a consignment like that would take its time to arrive. Everything came by sea to Thessaloniki. Then north through Macedonia.

I couldn't believe how many seeds we had. Seed mountain. I got some chogies to help and we tore the tops off the packets and poured the seed into buckets. Who cared if they stuffed their pockets too – good luck to 'em. Then it was time for some gardening. I've listened to *Gardeners' Question Time* – I know you're supposed to sow seeds at the proper depth, press them down with your thumb. Make sure they're fully watered, think loving thoughts the whole time, but we didn't do too badly just chucking them in bucketfuls out of the back of a Land Rover. It was a bit rough and ready. But it got the job done. Not too long before you could see the results. Strange stuff sprouting all over the place. There were flowers, plenty of flowers but there were also vegetables galore. Carters had treated themselves to a real old clear-out, dumping everything they had on us, which (to be fair) was just what I'd asked for. So you'd see little cabbages and baby marrows peeking out here and there, as well as poppies and petunias. The marrows wouldn't get to full size unless some madman with a watering-can or the only garden hose in Kosovo adopted them – your marrow like your melon is a thirsty brute. It wasn't the Chelsea Flower Show, but it was no end of an improvement. Christ knows anything that drew a bit of a veil over Pristina, leaves or flowers and whatnot, was doing everyone a favour.

After that I got a bit bomb-happy, firing off begging letters to anyone I could think of. I didn't spell it out that sending us surplus stuff was good publicity for them, but people aren't stupid. If there wasn't publicity to be had along the way, nothing much was going to travel up through Macedonia from Thessaloniki. I wrote to Penguin Books asking for old stock, and that was a letter I took a lot of care over. Fair few rough drafts and a fair copy. Book people – it stood to reason they would want proper spelling and grammar with not a hair out of place.

It worked. So they must have got some good press coverage out of it. A container of books made the trip. Then when I took a good look at what they'd sent I wondered whether they'd given a moment's thought to what soldiers would want to read or just gone into the warehouse blindfolded. I thought there would be some adventure. I mean, soldiering is supposed to be an adventure but nobody was getting much of that in Kosovo. Okay, maybe Penguin don't publish Andy McNab, but they must have something similar. They publish thousands of books, literally thousands. I still don't know whether they wanted to dump old stock, or whether they really thought servicemen on a peace-keeping mission in a war zone wanted to read that bloody big book. *War and Peace*. It must have been a joke, though, or am I taking the whole thing too much to heart? It was only a box of free books.

It was the other books in the container that bothered me more. I just couldn't see the lads reading them. The covers were all wrong, though it took me a while to work out why. The book covers didn't use photographs, just drawings – but they weren't professionally done drawings, they were spidery, and the lettering was the sort of thing you see on birthday cards, with lots of loops and squiggles. I'm trying to remember what was in those drawings. Iron garden furniture – a lot of that. Wine bottles, and cats. Straw hats. Sunglasses. I looked at all those books and I could feel them trying to tell me something, but I couldn't work out what it was.

Then one of the lads was standing behind me, and he got it in the instant. 'That's the sort of shit the wife likes,' he said. 'That's bloody chick lit, is what that is.'

They had sent servicemen and auxiliaries 'chick lit'. Of all things. But that's what they had sent us. Chick lit!

I spent even longer on the letter to Penguin complaining about those books than I did with the original letter, the one that asked for the books in the first place. Didn't want to get the writing wrong, badly needed to give Penguin a piece of my mind. Chick lit for squaddies – you can't get snottier than that, can you? And it's a good thing I took so long about it, all things considered. The next time I looked into the crate, the chick lit was gone. So maybe there was more to those books than the covers. Maybe Penguin knew their business after all. Still no takers for *War and Peace*, but the chick lit went like bloody wildfire. And maybe the lads went back to their wives with a better understanding of their hopes and dreams blah blah blah. Not something I'd bet on!

I went back on the warpath, sent a letter to Guinness, and didn't hear back from them, but somebody must have passed the message on to the competition, because Murphy's got in on the act and sent along two container-loads of their Millennium brew. Maybe there was an article I didn't see, a snidey item. About how Guinness didn't care about the British military contribution to NATO's presence in Kosovo – Murphy's having a greater understanding of the men serving over there, the men and their needs. It's all public relations, isn't it?

It was fine by me Murphy's taking the bait and not Guinness – I'd have felt differently if it was Caffrey's. I'd be tempted to tip the stuff away, or send it to the French with my compliments to make a nice winter shandy with the anti-freeze they were supposed to have hoarded. I had previous with the Corps of Royal Engineers, long before Kosovo, and previous with Caffrey's to boot. My first brush with the lads was when I was doing High Voltage/Low Voltage, not a refresher but actual training. Residential course, round mid-1990s time. Burn Hall near York. Cram cram cram, exam first thing Thursday morning. Wednesday night the lads set up a drinking competition. Of course they did! And I should have known better, I did know better. I absolutely knew better. Made no difference. This was a speed trial not an actual drinking contest, they said, and they convinced me I could handle it. It was a matter of who could drink the fastest, not the most, and I wasn't exactly young but still young enough to think I could swallow a few pints in double-quick time, gracious loser, respect all round, everybody's happy. Then I've got the rest of the evening to make friends with the water jug, piss away the pints, go to bed fresh. Wake up fresher, ready for the exam. Didn't happen.

It was Caffrey's we were drinking, made no difference to me, not as if you're going to be tasting much beer on a speed trial, drinking not tasting, just putting it out of sight as quick as you can. But as it turned out, did make a difference. Had to be Caffrey's if they were going to get me properly bamboozled. It was new in those days, Caffrey's, bit trendy, but that didn't have anything to do with what they were up to. Do the Yanks still say snafu and fubar? Snafu is Situation Normal All Fucked Up and fubar is the stage beyond. Fucked Up Beyond All Recognition. The lads wanted me fubar.

After the second or third pint it seemed that I was in the lead. The competition looked a bit green about the gills, and people were banging their fists on the bar and chanting *Baa-rry! Baa-rry!*. I'm not used to people cheering me on, haven't had a lot of that, and I suppose that was part of what got me bamboozled.

So I won the time trial, did a good job ignoring the celebratory pints people bought me, but I was still all over the place. Fell into bed, woke up dry, epic dry, and still drunk. Couldn't face breakfast, then it was time for the exam. Just about managed to scrawl my name on the paper, passed out. Someone gave me a good jab in the ribs, someone whispered, 'That's time, Barry,' in my ear and I came groggily awake and realized that was it, end of the time allotted. End of exam. The invigilator was collecting everybody's script. And I had nothing to give him. I hadn't made a mark, not one. Not a bloody mark. It was like the sort of dream that makes you wake up screaming. Except that in that sort of dream you don't look down and find that your exam paper has been filled in with all the right answers. In someone else's writing. The Saps had sabotaged me and then saved my bacon, shafted me then pulled my nuts out of the fire.

No-one likes to be on the receiving end of a prank, and I was surly as shit on the Friday, not to mention having a giant hangover to sleep off. The odd thing was that the Saps made me a bit of a pet after that. I was more popular with them after they'd made a total idiot of me than when they were urging me on with cries of *Baa-rry! Baa-rry!* Over breakfast on the Saturday, when I could just about look food in the face, they explained what they'd put over on me.

I had been concentrating on the wrong end of the process, and I was forgetting that the Engineers, guess what, are always likely to be engineering something. If I had been paying proper attention, I'd have noticed that the competition were getting pints that had been sitting for a minute or two, and I was being handed pints that had been under the tap seconds before. This being a time trial, I was chucking them down when they were still cloudy and swirling. It's all to do with the delivery system of Caffrey's. Not just carbon dioxide. Nitrogen. I'd been drinking those pints while they were still chock full of tiny bubbles, making for a creamy texture and a nice feel on the tongue, all of that, but doing me no bloody good at all. I wasn't just getting drunk, I was getting the bends, as good as. Alcohol poisoning with nitrogen narcosis on the side, poison chaser. Accelerant, petrol on flames. Far bloody cry from shandy. Potent as all hell. Not good!

So I had my reasons for knowing that the lads would get up to mischief, sure as eggs, if they weren't able to amuse themselves. Not bad lads – didn't they pull me back from the brink as well as get me fubar? But not schoolboys either or they would have let me alone to get my head around High Voltage/Low Voltage without giving me a heart attack in the exam room at the end of allotted time. And since that day, since that very day, not a drop of Caffrey's has passed my lips. Not from a keg, not from a can. You could produce a pint right there on the bar and have me watch over it until it was clear and flat, every atom of nitrogen gone from it. I still wouldn't feel a moment of temptation. I'd still tell you to push off.

Luckily it was Murphy's not Caffrey's we got sent so I didn't get too het up. Apparently there's a shot of whisky, or 'whiskey' I suppose it should be, being Irish, thrown in during the brewing process for the Murphy's Millennium brew. I have to say the lads wouldn't mind if there was a shot of cat sick added instead, just so long as the product as it finished up – product in its final form, chucked as intended down the neck of the end user – gave them the righteous hammering they had earned and were banking on.

The other times I'd made appeals for help were seen as a good thing by the powers that be, powers that were, but that delivery of Murphy's wasn't any too popular higher up. Not good for discipline, matter of fact. Naturally there's a mechanism that stops soldiers getting drunk. There would have to be, or our armed forces would fall apart and disgrace us in any country they were sent. It's called the Toucan Rule, and there's nothing much to it. It says, service personnel not permitted to drink more than two cans. That's it. Not complicated. Luckily it was still in force, even though there was a ton or so of free beer sitting there on base waiting to be pulled down below the point of no return, the Adam's apple of the lads. Only drawback is, the Toucan Rule is self-enforced. Not a matter of official discipline. So the brain that's meant to decide against the third can is ... do you see the flaw, the fatal flaw? Same old brain as said yes to the two before, isn't it?

Rodge, like me, being an attached civilian, wasn't subject to the Toucan Rule but we tried to limit his intake just the same. Beer gave him deep thoughts. Too deep. Not just *why are we in this bloody country?* More like *why are we even alive?* I think he had Irish blood, on his mother's side. It never got as bad as tears and old songs, but we kept a weather eye on him just the same.

Good publicity or no good publicity, there would have been no sense in Murphy's sending us their Millennium brew while it was still earning for them, so they must have sent it our way later, after the night when all the computers in the world weren't kaput after all, and everyone was a bit relieved and a bit disappointed. So I'm getting ahead of myself. Before the Murphy's, before the chick lit and even before the seeds Carters sent was all the really silly business, pranks and bets and dares. When we were really bored. Looking back at it, we spent a lot of time on stupid things. Arseing about. Pranks and dares, bets and forfeits, all of it coming under the heading of arseing about.

There are shed men and pub men, and I'm not saying one sort's better than the other, but it's handy if everyone in a group has the same priority. I almost said orientation! Get into a lot of trouble. I was a shed man and the lads were all pub. And the pub men didn't have a pub to go to, just the bar at BritFor Lines. Unless they fancied having a second run at the gangster place in town, which might not end up even as well as the first. And I didn't have a shed – workshop, yes, but that was work. When the lads downed tools they wanted to get hammered, but when I was finished for the day I still wanted a project to keep my hands busy. Getting hammered not being a project to my way of thinking. I just needed something to soak up spare energy before I could go to sleep.

As things worked in my marriage, while my marriage worked, well, Carol had her dressing room and I had my shed. I'm not going to pretend she asked for a dressing room but it seemed to me that between a couple everything has to be fair. If she had her dressing room then she couldn't complain about my shed. I wouldn't bother her in her dressing room and it was only polite for her to leave me alone in the shed. I had more square footage in what you'd have to call a shed-garage-workshop, and I won't pretend I didn't. But I used the shed for storing general supplies, things for the house, and in terms of space that could actually be used I reckon we were even stevens.

When things were bad we could have a bust-up about anything, even – can you believe – pizza. As if that could ever matter, but we managed it somehow. What's the worst fight you could have about pizza? Somebody doesn't like anchovies. Somebody doesn't like olives. If you don't like 'em, pick 'em off! You'd think that was about as heated as a pizza, let's say, dispute could get. Not even close! I come back from overseas for the boys' birthdays, yes from Kosovo, and I find Carol has booked us in to Pizza Hut. What's that about? How did it happen?

The boys wanted pizza. I understand that. I like pizza myself. In fact ... that's why I built the bloody great pizza oven in the garden. So why do we need to pay a visit to poxy Pizza Hut? Don't we have everything we need a hand's reach away? Ingredients for the dough, toppings, the whole lot?

The boys loved helping me build that oven. Loved it! Carol made out it was a typical Barry project, whatever that is, but everything about it was worked out with the boys in mind, from first idea to the final touch of magic, and it worked. It really worked. Undeniable. Matter of record.

Carol couldn't understand why there needed to be plans when all I was building was a pizza oven for the garden. I told her to wait and see. Banned her from the shed, saying it was a job for me and the boys. Fair play to her, she went along with the game, calling out to us when she was leaving mugs of juice and tea outside. The boys didn't quarrel, hardly made a peep, just watched as I worked.

Not always friends, those two, though that's what you hope for, isn't it? Got off to a bad start. George was, what, shy of two years old when Kevin comes along, and George was a bit delayed here and there. Walking fine, talking not so good. Nothing to worry about. Glue ear, as it turns out to be. Mostly the problem just goes away, but not with George, poor little beast – grommet needed putting in. And bad luck would have it, he gets it done the day his baby brother comes home from hospital. I took George up to Great Ormond Street, Carol's dad drove her home with the new arrival. Yes, men have their uses, even I have my uses, though she never wanted to admit it. Boy comes home from hospital and everything's different. One day, can't hear a thing. Silence. All alone in the world. Next day, sharing it with a howler monkey! Comes home all the way from Great Ormond Street – where, may I say, they treated him like a prince – with his hearing never better, only the present we've been telling him is such a treat, baby brother, is like a car alarm you can't shut off. Car alarm inside the house, blaring away. Healthy pair of lungs on Kevin, everyone's agreed about that.

Carol let me choose a name for our first. She was okay with 'George', and I didn't say why I chose it. Nice name, why not? If she decided it was what my dad was called, when she'd never met the man and never would, that was up to her. Then when she started telling her friends it was my dad's name I had to set her straight. Told her George was the name of my gaffer at Lesney's, long time ago, my last job as a tool cutter, 150 of us in a big room in Rochford. Nobody could set up a works outing like George. She wasn't impressed. 'What kind of man names his son after his gaffer from an old job?' she said. There should be a word for the answer you think of later, the zinger you couldn't lay hands on in the heat of battle. What I should have done was turn it back on her. Not difficult. 'What kind of man names his son after the dad he hasn't thought about for years?' How about that? That's good. But I never got the hang of the turning-things-around business. Just not how my brain works. I told her Lesney's were the people made Matchbox toys but that didn't help. After that I was excused naming duty! She named Kevin. Even with the boys' hamsters I didn't get a look in! Kevin wasn't her dad's name, maybe her grandad's, I didn't ask. Maybe an old boyfriend or a hairdresser who came up with a style that suited her. Didn't matter to me either way.

With the pizza oven most of the work was building the frame, plywood shaped into a dome. I wanted it trim and snug because that's my way, I can't pretend it made a huge difference, it's just a tidy finish being a habit you get into. Kevin didn't twig what I was doing, and said, 'Dad, if it's made of wood, won't it burn?' Yes, I told him, clever boy, you've got it in one. That's the fun part, and if you're really good I'll let you and your brother light the fire that burns it.

I enjoyed getting the boys acquainted with what I do, not the handy side of things so much as the brain work. There are things that seem silly when you try to explain them but make sense when you've seen them in practice. If you've only measured once you haven't measured at all – that sort of thing.

The brickwork for the plinth was plain sailing, and

then I used the dome to support the bricks for the oven proper. You could do it without a frame, I suppose, but it would be hell's own job. Then when the oven was built came time for the fun part. The touch of magic – the moment we set fire to the wooden dome inside the oven, now that it had done what it was made to do. The boys couldn't believe it was allowed. They hung back. They actually didn't dare to do it, so they left the job for me. It gave me a good laugh, that. I told them I wished they were like that on Bonfire Night. But their eyes were shining and even Carol joined in when they gave me a round of applause as the plywood burned away. The boys' own private pizza oven was all ready to start operations. To be honest, I'd rather build another whole pizza oven than make a single pizza from scratch, but that's just me. Get bases from Tesco and tart them up with toppings as you like, why not? That's more the style.

Carol took a picture of them gawping at the fire as it took hold, even if George didn't want it framed because it showed him with his thumb hovering just by his mouth. He'd pulled it out at the last moment before the picture was taken. Just when we thought thumb-sucking was something we'd seen the last of.

But when birthday time rolled around, different story. I'd warned the boys I couldn't come home for both birthdays, and it made sense to celebrate somewhere between the two dates – only a few weeks apart. Split the difference, but making it a Saturday, of course.

Carol told me the boys wanted to celebrate with pizzas, but not at home. They wanted to go to Pizza Hut. They're at an age when they want to fit in with their friends, she said. Don't you remember what that's like? I didn't really have an answer to that. Then I thought, Tell you what would make kids stand out anywhere, and that's having their own oven in the back yard and still going to bloody Pizza Hut. So I said it out loud. Said what I thought, can't always be a mistake can it? And Carol said, 'Barry, you're not the one scraping chocolate cake off the soles of twenty kids' shoes,' and then the penny dropped. It wasn't really the boys who wanted to go to Pizza Hut. But how were they going to tell me otherwise when their Mum had put her oar in, made up their minds for them? You can't expect that from kids. They wanted a quiet life, same as me, but we were all outvoted.

Carol could start a fight in an empty room – who said that? Her dear old dad, that's who. He had her number. Must have learned the hard way, same as me. Pizza wasn't even the high-water mark. There could be a fight about anything. Case in point, Carol comes to me, says what have you been telling George about pink toilet paper? That it's for poofs?

Well, I may not have said that, in so many words. I may have said 'poofy' but that's not much better is it? I'm old-fashioned, that's all it is. Maybe not up to date with the new ways of talking. I tried to explain to her. I've met gay people, got nothing against them, but still. We don't bother each other, just get on with our lives. I was a never a pretty boy. Not a disaster area, just not a pretty boy.

As for George or Kevin, or the pair of them, growing up gay, it's not something I'd want for my boys. Statement of fact. Fair enough, far as it goes. Not ideal. But if the boys decided to be gay, decided that's what they were, well good luck to them, I'd just warn them it wouldn't be plain sailing. It's easy for Elton John, it works for him, but he's not normal. You know what I mean! You know exactly what I mean. It's not a normal way of carrying on, spending that much on flowers. Hair sprouting on your head that's not yours. Works for him. It's not for everybody.

Carol could always beat me up in an argument. There was a always a knife handy when she wanted to be wounding. I told her I thought her friends didn't like me, they were always talking me down, and what does she say? It comes back right away, no need to think. *And how about* your *friends, Barry? Do they like me? Why don't you make some and let's find out.* Where was I supposed to start, dealing with that? I've got friends! The girls at Brize Norton liked me, didn't they? They send me Christmas cards, Sandra and Elly-with-a-y – and yes, I send cards back. Did I mention that I'm not stupid? In fact I send mine first. First week of December, bang them in the post. Don't want them thinking you only remembered them because they remembered you. It's hard to keep in touch when you're moving around a lot. There's some as can't stand their own company, and I'm not like that. Wouldn't have lasted so long if I was.

And for general information, my objection to pink toilet paper would be no different if the toilet paper was blue. Wouldn't have said 'poofy', granted – doubt if I'd still be married! I didn't care that the loo roll was pink – can't see how it matters. People don't have eyes in their ... enough said. Do I have to spell it out? Their arseholes. I just didn't see why Carol was buying fancy toilet paper when the shed was full of the stuff. Twelve dozen rolls! Enough to wipe an army. But she has to buy more. And all because there's a word written on the packaging of the rolls in the shed, and it's a word she can't stand.

Economy. I'd bought economy toilet paper, and why not? I don't mind so much spending money on other parts, other places, but that one? Don't see the need.

First major bit of silliness in Kosovo was Buzz and Woody running away together – same sort of messing about as goes on in civilian life. Garden gnomes take off to see the world and send their owners postcards from every faraway place you can think of. Ha ha. End up back on the lawn months later as if nothing had happened. Not even tanned, unless the joker who took them has given them a coat of varnish, finish off the prank in style. Civilian boredom is kid stuff – what do civilians have to get bored by? You get more mischief in the military. The Kosovo version was to do with two 'action figures'. That's what they want you to call dolls for boys. So these models were items of merchandising, film tat, displayed above the bar once upon a time in BritFor Lines, God knows why. *Toy Story*. Everybody goes soppy for that film. I don't get it, I just don't get it. Doesn't anyone grow up any more? Your toys don't care about you, never did, and by the way Santa Claus is your dad if you happen to have one around. Doesn't matter. End of rant.

So the idea was that Buzz – Lightyear, isn't it? – and Woody, who's some sort of cowboy, had run off together and one or other of them would give us an update about their adventures from time to time.

Buzz took me to a bar. We had a lot of beers. He said he wanted a woman. Two women. Three women. I said I just wanted to lie down. He got the wrong idea.

If the Powers had just ignored the prank it would have died down in no time at all, but no, the Powers had to get obsessed with putting a stop to such silliness. And then it was only going to get out of hand. Bloodymindedness. Point of principle.

I like it when Buzz is sweet to me. He has a tender side no-one else sees. I don't mind it so much when he bites the back of my neck, but I get scared when I see blood on the sheets. He keeps saying he promised his mother he would never pay for it. I don't understand. Pay for what? Laundry?

Stupid but a change from the normal order of business,

you have to admit. And you never knew when there would be a new instalment of the Buzz-and-Woody story, so it gave people an interest.

The Powers tried to crack down on the whole Buzz-and-Woody nonsense, but they hadn't given enough thought to strategy. How hard can it be to track down unauthorized transmissions, rogue broadcasts, on the military radio network? Harder than you'd think, when the transmitters are bouncing around in military vehicles in the first place, and mountainous terrain means the signal is being bounced around all over again by the relay stations that are needed to boost it. So the Buzz-and-Woody show had a good run for their money. It was mainly Woody doing the talking, and it all came out a bit strange.

Buzz wants me to wear a gingham dress like Cowgirl's. Of course I want to please him, but will he respect me if I do? He's sure it would suit me, though he says of course I'll need to lose weight. Does he even know how hurtful that is? I'm not so sure anyway, it's such an unflattering sack of a thing – but maybe I could cheer it up with a smart belt and a nice brooch.

What made it extra funny was that he didn't use a lispy voice – he said it the same way as announcing kit inspection or a foot patrol.

Buzz and I are on the rocks. Why can't he say he loves me? Just say it out loud. My mother was right – men are all the same. He only ever says one thing – 'Don't ask, don't tell' – and that's not enough for me any more. I can't stay with him now, not any more, though I don't know how I'll be able to carry on, after everything we've been to each other. But there comes a time when you have to draw a line in the sand. And he crossed that line. He forgot... I can hardly bear to think about it even now. I get so upset. He forgot my birthday.

That got a laugh from me, I don't mind saying. I was

doing the payroll round at the time, trickier job than it sounds. Very much an outward-bound assignment. Duke of Edinburgh would have been proud of me! Gold Award and a bit more. I wasn't in a post room slipping envelopes into pigeonholes, whistling and looking forward to my tea. I was fighting to control my vehicle on the way to one of our other bases, driving along a road that was all ruts of ice. Choose your rut, hope it sees you right. Official perception of the bank in Pristina was that it was as secure as a toddler's money box, and we didn't hang around there, just withdrew the cash and scarpered. I'd sort it into envelopes on base and then set out on my delivery round.

I was still laughing at Woody's moan about birthdays when a vehicle behind started sounding its horn. Stroppy. But what was I supposed to do? I couldn't pull over with the road in the state it was – I might never get traction again – and I wasn't going to discuss the matter with a bunch of the locals at a time that the Land Rover was bursting with cash. The amounts were counted out and the name or nickname of the designated chogie was written painstakingly on each envelope. There was no security for the payroll run – unless thick rubber bands count as security! I used them to hold the batches of envelopes together. So I wasn't going to back down. Had to keep going. Long story short – guns waved around but not fired. Lucky escape. I didn't have a gun, of course. As for me, sphincter tight, *mighty* tight, but not letting me down. Hanging in there, as they say. It's only afterwards I think about getting killed and how easily it could have happened. Country still in the shit after there was killing everywhere, killing out of hand, killing for killing's sake. What's one more? Foreigner, attached civilian. And me not killed for envelopes full of Deutschmarks piled up in the passenger footwell, but in a general way. For being in the wrong place at the wrong time and getting some-one pissed off. I still don't see what else I could have done, and if I was in the wrong place at the wrong time then we all were.

But that wasn't what I was talking about. I've got sidetracked. Women and birthdays. All right, so I for-got one birthday – one. I thought we were meant to be more grown-up than that. Squabbling about what's not important. I remembered the boys, didn't I? January the 17th, May the 18th. Not difficult, I admit, for anyone that knows anything about the battle of Monte Cassino, though I couldn't exactly say that to her. Why couldn't she have a birthday like the boys' ones, something that was easy to remember? It wasn't going to be in the forefront of my mind, was it, seeing as how I was attached to a NATO peace-keeping mission policing a ravaged hellhole at the time. That's right, attached to a peace-keeping mission in a hellhole. Other things to think about. I had no end of things to do. There are some things people just can't take in, however many times you say them. But these are the things that people ought to consider before they decide they're being badly treated. I'm not a hypocrite. Miss my birthday and see if I turn a hair. Sauce for goose, sauce for gander. With kids it's different, I can see that, and I never missed one. George and Kevin – I didn't forget my boys' birthdays. Never will.

So how about a sense of proportion? Rodge's wife has a breast cancer scare, and he stays put – nobody thinks he's letting her down. Doesn't make him a monster. She gets the all clear, big bunch of flowers, life goes on.

I know what you're thinking – I should have married Mrs Rodge! Couldn't say. Never met the lady.

When I went into the little box office once, to phone Carol after I'd missed her birthday in fact, there was a rank smell in there, really sharp. Smelt like a hedge that's just been cut – not a lot like air freshener! Not air freshener by a long chalk. I could see a wad of tissues, just dropped on the floor. Not much of a secret. Some squaddie had only been treating himself to a lovely old wank while he chatted to the missus. Imagine that.

After that, when I was actually talking to Carol, I couldn't concentrate. My mind wandered. I don't mind saying it made me feel a little bit sick, the mess on the floor. Put me right off my stride, and I couldn't explain to Carol why I was feeling out of sorts. 'You'll never guess what I just found,' I said. 'What have you found, Barry? Get on with it. Say your piece. I've got things to do even if you don't.' That was pushy! I found it hard to talk, harder than usual, even. Which I didn't think was possible. Very tongue-tied, I was, but I don't expect it made a difference. She wanted to tell me what a bad time this was to talk, how inconvenient for her – when wasn't she the one who picked it in the first place? I was being punished for forgetting the birthday, of course. No point in apologizing. Apologies cut no ice with Carol.

General idea – I didn't need to be in Kosovo. My family needed me, she needed me. I had no business being so far from home. There was a word she couldn't seem to take in. *Mission*. NATO peace-keeping mission in a hellhole. Something to be kept in mind. Part of the picture. In fact the whole of the picture. My job. Though yes, of course, if you're going to take her side, I didn't need to be there. Not in the way the forces did. But once I was there I had to stay there. In much the same way that they did. I wouldn't be court-martialled if I ran off, true, but I'd be in plenty of other sorts of trouble, civilian trouble. Not to mention no money coming in. How is that *playing at soldiers*? What she said.

That was the conversation between spouses, while we were still 'spouses', and I didn't get a lot out of it. So I hope she felt better after she'd had her say. After I'd left the cabin, of course, I got worried that someone might think the mucky wad was my doing. Nothing I could do about that. I'd have thrown it away if I could but then I'd need to touch it, wouldn't I?

By the time her birthday came round again, I'd bodged up a way of remembering it – Tobruk minus two. Two days before it began, the Siege of Tobruk. But by then I was only supposed to contact her through her lawyer, and things were bad enough between us without my getting on her nerves even more than I had already. I hadn't seen the boys for a while. So I sent my card 'care of' her lawyer and asked him to make sure she got it.

Once in a blue moon she'd ask me something by the same route, through the lawyer. Silly stuff, not important. As a for instance – how was she supposed to get the wardrobes out of the bedroom? Couldn't be done, without smashing them up. Only MFI, but not going anywhere after I'd nailed and glued them. Bigger than the bedroom doors, so smash 'em up! Enjoy yourself. That's what I told her.

Kosovo was a tough test all round but I wouldn't have missed it. Fell in love with the NATO hitch, for one thing. Universal coupling – no better way of attaching a trailer or anything else that needs towing. Back in Britain I had a car run into the back of mine – not just a graze, not a matter of *so sorry*, exchange details, pain in the arse but just one of those things. Full-on impact while I was stationary, minding my own business. Bang! To give you some idea, radio flew backwards from its housing. Found it on the back seat afterwards.

Clear-cut situation for the insurers, though – small

mercies. No quibbles. That's what I thought anyway, then when they rebuilt the back of the car, no NATO hitch. Now if you've ever tried a NATO hitch you won't go back to standard. They're like night and day. *Big* difference. NATO hitch gives you movement in three dimensions, much easier life on rough terrain. So it was a case of going to claims court and forcing the insurers to install what I wanted – what I had before. NATO hitch. Thank you very much. Don't make it so hard next time, or pick on someone who doesn't know his rights.

I could have taken her to court, the driver, but what's the point? Bit embarrassing anyway. Apparently she hadn't finished saying her piece. I'd heard enough. Walked away. Got in the car. Was just about to drive away, when *Bang!* And no, I wasn't two-timing anyone, this was after my marriage and I wasn't playing the field. This was a lady who thought there was more going on than there was. Nothing to discuss.

I've learned the hard way that it's simpler to say I was never married, never had children, best not go into the whole sad story. Keep things simple. Fresh start, why not?

And if she thought, this lady, that she was going to get my attention by crashing into my car before I had a chance to drive off, well in a way she was right. She got my attention but that's not the same as listening, is it? Not when I was looking at the place my NATO hitch used to be. So she didn't get value for money, to my way of thinking. Chucked away her no-claims bonus, sod all to show for it.

Wouldn't have minded a bit of whiplash – little bit – for extra leverage from an insurance angle. Turns out I'm a bit limber, just bounce back. Can't be helped!

In Kosovo I saw some dodgy moments and some glorious soldiering. British troops advancing on a rioting crowd with their shields up, moving as one man, after the French turned tail. I could show you pictures I took. Magnificent! I've seen squaddies doing their duty, head down and no questions asked, but I've also seen officers making up their own minds. Finding their way out of tricky situations. Initiative. Rarest thing in a military setting. Same as hands just automatically salute, soldiers don't stop saying Yes just because they think No. Hardly surprising there's a shortage of initiative when it's been drilled out of soldiers from their first day. Drilled out of 'em – it sounds like a dentist going to town on civvy character, grinding it down. Most of the time it might as well be.

A captain by the name of Blunt got a lot of respect for the way he interpreted his orders. Interpreting orders! That would be a new idea for most military. Creativity. This was before I got there, so if we were the first wave then Blunt was in the wave before that. James B was in the Life Guards when he volunteered for deployment with the Blues and Royals, so he was sent over to our neck of the woods. And then his unit was ordered to take the airport, Pristina airport, from the Russians, who had just happened to get there first. The order came from NATO's American commander, so this young man was supposed to get cracking with a superpower showdown. Just what the world needed. I don't know what was going through his head – maybe that if the Yanks wanted a war they should at least fire the first shot themselves. Anyway, they handed him a battle and he gave them a blockade instead. He didn't stop the Russians getting to the airport, he sat on his hands and then he sealed them inside it. So there was stalemate and not showdown. Brilliant! That counts as a victory. 'The Russians' makes them sound like an army, when there were only about 200 of them, but they were supposed to stop at the border and the world was watching, 'the world was watching', meaning a few tired journalists, no disrespect to Miss Adie, trying to blow everything up into a crisis.

They were still talking about it when I arrived in the country. It was beautiful, and I think of that every time I hear his song, the one that was a big hit. 'Beautiful'. Though it's not my favourite tune by a long chalk. He hadn't written it then, or maybe he had. Maybe he sang it to his unit every night to get them to sleep, but it wasn't a record then. What do I like to listen to? Tony Bennett. Sinatra before he spent all his time with gangsters. Willie Nelson before he smoked too much dope. Lovely way with a melody. Heartfelt. Not that I'm much of a collector. Doubt if I've got more than a dozen CDs all told. If I'm ever asked to do *Desert Island Discs*, I won't need long to make up my mind. I could do it in ten minutes from a standing start. I might even play 'Beautiful', just to tell the interviewer lady about James Blunt and the airport blockade. I suppose I'd better add a woman to the list so listeners don't think I'm strange. Gracie Fields! 'If I Knew You Were Comin' I'd've Baked A Cake', why not? That's a joke. I quite like Tammy Whatnot when she sang about divorce. At least she sounded as if she thought marriage was for keeps! That's another joke. What I should really do is make all my discs the theme tunes of old radio programmes. That's what brings your life back. Not the programmes, just the theme tunes.

I went to a Fathers For Justice meeting, just the one, after the divorce and when I told them what had happened they said I needed to take the gloves off, fight for my boys. I hadn't done enough. I'd let Carol walk all over me.

I didn't go back there. One meeting was enough. They were all angrier than I was, and I didn't want to be angry in the first place. Hate it. Fighting for my boys would be no different than fighting them plain and simple. Then someone asked about my family background. Had my parents stuck together? After that I couldn't leave fast enough. They shouldn't have asked. I hadn't forgotten! Hadn't forgotten that I'd let a bad thing happen all over again. I knew what it'd do to the boys, which Carol didn't. She wouldn't listen. A mum's the most important person. Well, I go along with that, early on. Early on in life. Didn't I make sure George and Kevin remembered Mother's Day? But did the boys even know when Father's Day is? Okay, not the best example. All that rubbish is made up by marketing people, and I don't know myself. But one thing I do know – a mum can't help a boy grow up all by herself.

The boys always knew how I felt, and if they didn't how would it have helped to drag them back and forward between us? They know how to find me. They'll get in touch when they're ready. Sooner or later they'll work out they haven't heard the whole story. There's a whole piece missing from their lives.

Our boys had some fun, while the Russians were stuck in the airport, rolling tyres their way from our positions in the middle of the night. They make a hell of a lot of noise bouncing downhill, and you have to have pretty strong nerves when you're on the receiving end not to think you're under attack. Was it part of our strategy? No, our lads were just mucking about, same as soldiers have always mucked about. It's a way of coping, and if you're civilian attached to the military you're likely to be roped into the mucking about along with everything else. I don't know whose idea it was to race across Lake Batlava, round trip, to the island and back, it was probably the ranks, but Rodge and I didn't make much of an objection. We were all of us set up by the lake with a fair amount of kit – we weren't on leave – and the weather was nice, but the Saps were waiting for their orders on a retrieval operation and none of us was expecting to be having fun any time soon. Some sort of mucking around was inevitable. Sooner or later someone was going to make a bet on something, and it just happened to be racing across Batlava Lake. Or rather – not a bet.

Not a bet, because there are regs against that. It was a forfeit ... same thing but the other way round, and gets round the disciplinary side of things. No rules against forfeits. So it wasn't the first team to the funnel and back that won a bet, it was the last team there and back who had to pay a forfeit. 300 Deutschmarks. Not a fortune, not enough to retire on, but you wouldn't want to drop that much if you could avoid it by putting in a little effort.

It was a gentleman's agreement, and you have to watch out for those. Odds on you find it's not gentlemen you're dealing with. The lake race an absolute bloody case in point. Gentlemen would have reminded Rodge and me that we'd signed a bit of paper agreeing to the bet, to the forfeit, which we'd done one evening when the self-enforced two-can rule had not been enforced by any of the parties involved. Technically the two-can rule didn't apply to me anyway, but common sense did. Should have, anyway.

It was only after a day or two of hard-to-get jokes – references to Cunard and the White Star Line, that sort of thing – that we woke up to the fact we were committed to amateur boatbuilding against the clock. Turned out we'd signed a piece of paper. A sort of contract between 'Members of the Corps of Royal Engineers on retrieval duty at Batlava Lake' and – wait for it – 'Barry's lot'. Bloody hell! That's rude. That's needling. But of course that was all part and parcel of what they were up to. It was obvious that the Engineers, the Sappers, the Measurers, the Mudlarks, the Mounted Bricklayers, call them what you will, had fallen in and made a start on something spectacular. Perhaps they didn't even go to sleep, the night we all signed up to the bloody forfeit, but made a start sawing planks. Or making sketches. For their mahogany panelling, God save us.

That was the twist, the fun part of the forfeit, I suppose – that we had to build our own boats. And we'd lost some time. I had one or two ideas, just the same. I didn't mind putting in a bit of effort. Short-cuts, hoping to make up some ground. Sort of pre-fab approach. Most of what I'd done in Kosovo was modular, all the bases were modular. My brain was modular! Probably.

There was a chance they'd get bogged down in some finicky job, caulking or whatnot, and *Barry's lot* could sneak a cheeky lead, on the construction side of things at least. The race itself I gave up on long before it happened. Not my area of excellence, though I did a bit of kayaking back in the misty past. Rodge no great shakes either from what he said. He'd hired a pedalo a few times! And that was it. We'd draft in a couple of sparks or plumb bobs to round out the crew. Crew! Some hope. One would need to be my size and one Rodge's, to make for some rough approximation of balance. I just prayed we put up a reasonable show, or else accepted being laughing-stocks without too much bad grace. There was always a chance the lads would be laughing so hard we'd make it to the funnel and back before they'd got their rhythm at the oars. If their craft was too fancy they might be the losers in terms of power-to-weight. Then we might dodge the early bath that was waiting for us.

We were the underdogs from the start, and sometimes

the underdog needs to do the clever thing and not bother. Creep off to the kennel, lick your arse till you feel better, have a good nap. The Saps had the facilities – they could build their bloody boat in a base that wasn't a shipyard, no, but had most of any equipment they'd need. They had the wherewithal. Then they could load their boat onto a bloody big truck. We had to do everything at the little camp we'd set up by the lake, bring our materials there in Land Rovers and hope we'd not forgotten something vital.

The ranks were very secretive about what they were doing in their base, but they kept coming over to our little camp to take a look at what we were doing, and trying to keep a straight face when they saw it. What were we doing? We were bolting a couple of shower cubicles together, end to end. Cutting away the panels that joined, of course, but that was basically it. That was the hull of our sturdy craft, that was what we were relying on to earn us 300DM, or saving us from paying out 300DM, which – for anyone at the back who hasn't been paying attention – comes to the same thing.

Was it seaworthy, sorry, lakeworthy? Sort of. Stretching a point. The first time we had it in the water, muggins here was volunteered to be test pilot. Lighter than Rodge, a lot lighter, but I'm not sure that was the real issue. Rodge was a lot more sensible, and really I could see the flaws myself even if I didn't want to own up to it. I'd got some chogies to rustle us up a couple of oars, shaping some blades to fasten onto broomsticks, which I suppose was cheating but the rules of the forfeit weren't exactly signed and sealed with blobs of wax and lodged with Lloyds of London. We were happy with what we'd decided to call our boat, though looking back I don't know why we thought we'd come up with such a cracker of a name.

HMS *Weelfookem*. Painted on the side of the shower-cubicle hull. Nothing to stop us spelling it out as We'll Fuck 'Em, which was what was meant, but I didn't quite have the nerve come painting time.

I'd been toying with another name, but I wasn't sure how I'd explain it to Rodge. The *Stig of the Dump*. It would have suited our ramshackle bit of construction. Then when Rodge said, 'We need a strong name – a fuck-off name,' that was the end of the line for Stig. Stig got dumped on the spot.

The 'oars' were pretty pitiful, and we'd jury-rigged rowlocks out of plastic ties. If there's a way to shave a block of expanded polystyrene into a comfy cushion for a person's bum while he's trying to give his all as an oars-man in a race to catch up with 300DM – or, this being a forfeit, to prevent minus 300DM from catching up with him – then I hadn't managed to find it in the time available. I fixed the seats in place with plenty of super-glue. Superglue the bodger's friend. Whatever did we do before superglue? Cursed the makers of Bostik and Araldite, that's what, for making us wait around for pathetic results. Half-hearted apology for the bonding of materials. Fixed seats were obviously mechanically inefficient, disastrous, a bad joke, but we were under the cosh – and it wasn't the Oxford and Cambridge Boat Race, was it? There were limitations. We didn't aim as high as sliding seats, to get maximum power from each stroke. That wasn't an option on the *Weelfookem* Mk I, and there wasn't going to be a *Weelfookem* Mk II as far as I was concerned, win or lose.

I clambered aboard and it wobbled – as the lads say – like holy fuck, but I sat myself down and made a grab for the oars while Rodge gave the *Weelfookem* an almighty push and for about five seconds everything seemed to be all right. If I'd been able to grab the oars properly and get an even stroke going I might have been able to keep the whole thing in balance, even on my own, but it was hopelessly unstable and I ended up just where I didn't want to be, in the waters of Lake Batlava. Not cold, not in the hot time of year. Another time even a refreshing dip. Still, I managed to keep my head out of the water and Rodge pulled the 'boat' back to shore with me clinging on to it, not having a good time and not pretending to.

When I was back on dry land Rodge wasn't sympathetic, in fact he did his best to get at me. Couldn't help himself. Weren't we teammates? Didn't make a difference. He sniffed the air and said, 'Do you smell that?' I told him there was no smell. There was no smell. Clear about that. I could have done without Rodge mucking about just then.

We needed to address the stability issue, and there were only hours to go before the race itself. We were going to have to take a leaf out of the book of anyone down the ages who didn't have a lot in the way of technical resources but didn't want to capsize. We would use outriggers. Not sure I can really call them outriggers! Ours were made of lengths of plastic soil pipe capped off with whatever we had handy. I'd have used jam jar lids if I'd had to, sticky-backed plastic even. More *Blue Peter* territory than *Jane's Fighting Ships*, kiddies' telly level, not very grown-up, but when it came down to it that was just too bad. This was a silly project that had a serious side. Race against the clock but no special treatment. I would have downed tools except I'm not made that way. I didn't want to pay the forfeit, goes without saying, plus I didn't want to end up in the water again. One dip plenty to be getting on with. But it's more than that. Once I've got a project I stay with it. It's stronger than me. Things need to get finished – it's not up for negotiation. It needs to happen. I need it to happen.

Zero hour for the forfeit, and along comes the Saps' truck. They kept us waiting to see what we were up against. There was a sort of unveiling ceremony, touch of theatre. They formed up in two lines at the back of the truck, and we waited for the doors to open. They looked pretty silly – wearing wellingtons and shorts. Then some music starts. Music! They're really trying to show us up. Fanfare – of a sort. Weird-sounding. Not a recording, nor a proper instrument neither, bugle or whatnot ... turns out one of them is playing a kazoo. Kind of thing falls out of a Christmas cracker, kids love it. After half an hour an adult accidentally steps on it. Sighs of relief. The Sap with the kazoo is trying not to crack up as he tootles into it, makes it sound even weirder. Meanwhile – I'd not noticed – two of the others have empty paint tins slung round their waists, drummer-boy style. Different sizes, different notes when they hit them with bits of dowelling.

Pom-pom-*pom*-pom-*pom*-pom-*pom*-pom-*pom*.   Then the fanfare begins again. Film theme. You'd know it if you heard it. Outer space.

First thing out of the back of the truck wasn't a boat at all. It was a barbecue – not quite industrial-size. Pretty hefty just the same. Gas canister. After that, big boxes of meat to cook on it. Sausages and burgers, buns. Big dispensers of tomato sauce and salad cream. So we knew we were going to have a change from the chogie cooking on base, win or lose. Was there any veg to go with the meat? Was there any salad? No there was not.

What did you say your name was – Linda McCartney?

Well, there was coleslaw, in tubs, but I'm never sure what coleslaw is or why it's there. I don't like it, don't see the point of it. Is it a vegetable? Are there vegetables in it? Out of the truck came big plastic chests that made a bit of a sloshing and a clinking while they were being man-handled, so we knew that cold beer had been laid on too. The ranks weren't allowed to buy beer from the stores, the way we civilians were, but they'd found a way round that. When the Saps want a party, there's no stopping them. If you don't want to join in, you'd best get out of the way. They were hell-bent on having a good time, but I don't think anyone was in the mood, deep down. If you're having fun you don't have to keep saying 'Isn't this fun?' which was pretty much the mood of the whole group.

Once, when I was working for Lesney, our gaffer George arranged a day out for all of us. Train to Blackpool for the day – early start. He hadn't just booked tickets for us, he'd chartered a whole bloody train. Direct to Blackpool. No other stops. While we were waiting on the platform he turned up driving a little motorized cart. It was pulling a whole string of little trucks behind it, piled high with beer crates. Now *that's* a works outing! Race across Batlava Lake didn't come close. No real joy in it.

Finally the boat came out of the back of the truck into the sunlight, wheeled down the ramp on a trailer, but it was all wrapped up in tarpaulins. Couldn't see much. Even so it had us beaten already. It looked like a boat! That made it the winner. The lads wanted to keep the suspense going a while longer, make us suffer. The music detail formed up again, did their bit one more time with the fanfare and the *pom*-pom-*pom*-pom-*pom*. Rodge growled at me, 'This is like a fucking strip show,' and shouted out 'Get 'em off! Get 'em off! Show us yer bits!' Playing a part.

They were having a game with us, but they got the message in the end and pulled the tarps clear, to show off what they had built. It wouldn't have won prizes at a boat show, true enough. The varnish on it wasn't dry, but that helped it to sparkle. And it had a proper frame, plywood panels. Nice curve to them. Of course they could get their hands on any amount of kit, at no expense. We could only use what we had in our stores. Slim pickings. Then bodge it together by the lake. They could hide what they were doing, tucked safe away in the Motor Transport building back at base, proper steel frame like a Tescos back home. What they'd built looked like an actual boat – it didn't look like a couple of messed-about shower cubicles. Then Rodge gave me a nudge and flicked his eyes towards the side of the Saps' boat, meaning get an eyeful of that. They'd stencilled the name up there.

I got an eyeful of it, more than I was ready for. The *Gloria Du Cunt*, that's what they'd called their boat. Which I thought was pretty strong. A bit close to the bone. They certainly made us seem pretty timid with our *Weelfookem*. Not having the nerve to spell out what we meant. Rodge muttered that they made us look like pussies, not meaning little cats, and he had a point ... they'd shown us their bits.

They'd shown us their bits! It would have been a good moment to concede the forfeit, to say *Well done, lads. You've made your point. Fine piece of work, lovely craftsmanship. Here's your 300DM and by the way it's my round. . .what can I get you?* But no short cuts – we had to take our punishment, get dropped in gunge, take our chances with the gunk dunk. Like in *Get Your Own Back* – now that was a programme that really grabbed my boys. Kids being teamed up with parents or teachers they had scores to settle with, then playing games with messy forfeits. Mad really – what twisted mind came up with that? But Kevin loved it, gave a whoop every time a grown-up got dunked in slime. George wasn't so sure, though he couldn't stop watching. He couldn't really believe it was allowed.

80

The Saps lifted their boat off the trailer and marched it into Batlava Lake. The music detail fell in and helped move it. The *Weelfookem* was already in the water, and it might have been at the bottom of the lake already for all the chance it had against the *Gloria D*. There was a count-down – *ten! nine! eight!* – and we got a move on when it went down to *zero*, so we were the first off the mark. The Saps took their time. Giving us a head start, maybe, just to rub it in. They had so much of an advantage they hardly needed to bother.

The music detail, the Saps with the kazoo and the drums of paint, they didn't get on board after the launch. Stayed by the side of the lake giving the rowers a rhythm, the drummers doing most of the work, naturally. *Stroke! Stroke!* Different film now, you'll notice. Not outer space and aliens, more sea battles and blokes in togas. Galley slaves.

We weren't chained to the oars, no. Didn't mean we could get out of it. Rodge and me had to go through with the forfeit, give the ranks their fun. Not to mention the others, the poor sparks and plumb bob we'd roped in, tell-ing them it would be a break from routine. Fun day out! There's always enough gunge to go round. The two of them'd gone a bit green when they'd seen the *Weelfookem*. We'd sold the race to them over some beers at BritFor Lines, and it would take a lot more beers after the race, solid weeks of beers, to make them forget they'd been had.

Stroke! Stroke! On board the *Weelfookem* we try to match their pace, but after a few strokes we're just cream-crack-ered. Fighting for breath – not just me, Rodge feels it too – and wondering if we're going to throw up just to make the day even more fun.

They fell behind. Stopped giving it their all. And we slacked off a bit – human nature – thinking we were going to be 300 Deutschmarks to the good, though there seemed to be no rhyme or reason. Then what? Sound of an engine starting up, tinny little two-stroke, smell of petrol drifting across to us. What's happening? They're cheating by using an engine, that's what's happening. Bang out of order! I mean, getting chogies to lend a hand with the oars is one thing. Not quite right, I'm not pretending any different. Borderline, and maybe the wrong side of borderline. Crossing over into naughty. But using an engine when the forfeit said *under own power* – as many words – is another. Clear violation.

Except they weren't using the engine for power. They were playing a different game. They had slowed down so we'd have a clear view of them when they opened fire. It came towards me, this jet of water, and yes it also came towards the sparks beside me but it was me it hit. I was the target. My hands went up to protect my glasses and the water jet punched me in the chest. Solar plexus. Hit me like a fist. Plenty of power there. Caught me off balance and I dropped my oar. I could do a diagram of the forces operating – textbook. I was driven backwards, and Rodge to my rear ... well, either he tried to catch me or he was wanting to tuck himself away safe behind me. Might have worked if he'd stuck to it, though I'm on the small side for duty as a human shield, but then he dropped his oar too, half stood up to make a grab for it, and then the forces were well and truly out of kilter. No diagram needed!

The other two oarsman clung on when Rodge and I, well ... left the boat. My hands had gone down from protecting my glasses when the water jet hit me in the chest but now they went up again. Risky strategy but better than no strategy at all. Skinned my elbow on the way down.

The Saps had waited until we were in deep water. Of course they had! No fun in winning the forfeit without giving us maximum possible grief. They showed their class as opponents, did the Saps. And Rodge and I showed our class as castaways by trying to clamber back aboard from the same side of the *Weelfookem*. If we'd given it a bit of thought one of us would have swum round the other side, and then if we timed it carefully there was a chance of the boat – I have to go calling it 'boat', don't I? – staying upright despite the weight differential. But we just wanted to get out of the water as soon as possible. We were trying to join the other two, and they joined us instead. Did nothing wrong and still ended up in the lake with the pair of us. So the Saps got a bonus on top of winning the forfeit, full house of attached civilians given the gunk dunk treatment. All of us spluttering in the water.

We stayed where we were, holding on to the *Weelfookem*, keeping our mouths above the surface. Nobody was coming to pick us up any time soon. The Saps in *Gloria D.* were going to finish the circuit that fulfilled the forfeit, camp to funnel and back, but they weren't in any hurry. Pleasure trip.

I tried to say, *this isn't all bad. Just imagine you're on a Club 18–30 break, sun's out, water's not too cold, there's a barbecue in the offing, plenty of beer ... I mean. It could be worse.* Mainly for the benefit of the other two, the sparks and the plumb bob. Rodge wasn't having it. 'We're not trained for this,' he said. 'It's different for the ranks. Sappers get training for shit like this.'

I said at least we were safe from sharks. Didn't go down well. And I thanked my stars that I hadn't lost my glasses, though I kept that to myself. Unlikely to give the others a massive boost. I'm not helpless without them. Struggle a bit when I'm tired. My skinned elbow felt sore but I've had worse. Tried to keep it raised out of the water. I'd put some antiseptic on it later.

At least we didn't have blisters – no time for that! Hardly touched the oars.

I asked Rodge if he could smell anything. Couldn't resist it! 'Fuck me, Baz,' he said. 'I knew you wouldn't let me forget that. Of course there's no smell.' I didn't say any different.

Music started to reach us. Wonderful how sound carries across water. Kazoos again – more than one. Whole kazoo chorus. There were, what, six Saps on the *Gloria D.* and they all brought one along. Job lot, maybe, from Pristina market. Turned out they were all musicians! Different tune, too, bit less po-faced. Classic song, too. Hymn tune, good as. 'Vindaloo'. Gets on your brain. You don't need to hear the words to hear the words, if you see what I mean. Would they *score one more* than us? They already did. Cheeky sods, having their lap of honour before they'd even finished the race! *Where you come from, do you put the kettle on?* Catchy as anything, but you can't really tap your toes when you're treading water.

Did they pick us up, or at least give us a tow, on the return trip? Fat chance. They probably guessed one of us would take a swing at them – maybe all of us. Get our own back. Take command of the *Gloria D.*, snatch back the forfeit. So we stayed there stranded a while longer, until they could be arsed to come and fetch us. We weren't cold when they fished us out, not a bit. Bit of shivering just the same.

'Barry's lot' were pretty done in. Even so, I thought we should keep busy, take the *Weelfookem* apart again, stow the pieces in the Land Rover. Long wheelbase but not exactly the Tardis. Not that I had plans to take a couple of hacked-up shower cubicles to Pristina market. Swop 'em for a box of kazoos! It just made sense to keep ourselves to ourselves for a while. Keep our heads down. We needn't be in a hurry to get to the barbecue. We'd be in for a few hours of showing what good sports we were. Taking it on the chin – 'sucking it up' is the thing people say nowadays.

After a while the smell of barbecue made us think – well, I'm speaking for myself here – maybe it wouldn't be all bad. Not all bad. Who doesn't like roast meat, bangers and burgers? Burn your mouth and ask for seconds.

The man in charge of the meat was Micky. That's the Sap who didn't think you could get hitched for less than a hundred grand – and got just a little stroppy when I didn't agree. Good mood on him now, though. There's a word for it, mag-something ... got it! Magnanimous. Micky was being magnanimous in victory. He was loving it.

'Anyone like their meat rare?' he said, playing a flame-thrower over meat that was already sizzling. 'If so, speak up ... and I'll tell you you're at the wrong fucking barbe-cue, mate.' It actually was a flamethrower he was holding. The Saps think big, but Rodge and I knew that already from the big shiny boat. And the water cannon.

Barbecues give guys a Stone Age feeling, without a doubt. Like old Fred Flintstone with his Bronto-burgers. Primitive, meat and fire, so beat your chest. Chuck in a flamethrower and everyone's a caveman. Doesn't take me that way. I'll queue for a hot dog like a good little boy.

I had to take things on the chin right away. Suck it up. Don't give me a burger first, just start rubbing it in. Micky filled me in about the race and how it ended the way it did. 'Proper boat needs a woman's name,' he said. 'That's what went wrong with the *Titanic*. Sank like a stone. HMS *Hood*, same thing. Blew up like an arsehole.' He gave a belch. 'Well-known fact. Proper boat needs a woman's name.' Not sure calling our bodged-up shower cubicles the *Lady Weelfookem* would have swung the race our way, but no point saying so. Bad loser. Not a name you want.

'Plus we had value added,' he said, 'from the motto.' I didn't know what he meant – I'd forgotten the motto of the Engineers. I was allowed a little forgetting, wasn't I? There wasn't a lot of the day that wanted remembering, and it wasn't over yet. Turns out the motto's in Latin, goes something something *gloria ducunt*. And that's where she came from, good ship *Gloria Du Cunt*. Glory is leading the Saps somewhere, that's the idea – do they know where? Christ knows. And if Rodge and I had a motto I don't know what it would be. Maybe *Can we fix it? Yes we can!* Motto of Robertus the Builderus, not to mention Rodge, bodging for England, and Barry. Barry well out of his depth. This time we couldn't fix it. It wasn't glory leading us, that's for sure, not on the maiden voyage of the *Weelfookem*.

I asked about the water cannon. Something I needed to know. Was it a last-minute thing, drop a hose over the side, or the first thing they thought of? 'Whole point of the boat, mate. Proper water intake, pump in the hull.' They were entitled to say hull, I suppose, which we weren't, not really. Got me thinking. That was their first idea, drenching me. The others were on their list, yeah, but I was at the head of it. That's what it was all about, under the surface.

It wasn't water pressure that powered that jet – well, obviously it was the water pressure. But in another way it was something else. One-way salutes. There must have been thousands of them. Every one the lads had given and not got back. When you think about it, there were thousands of backed-up salutes powering that water cannon to knock me off the *Weelfookem* and into Batlava Lake.

There only one thing that made Micky and the other Saps look like idiots, almost more than we did. In the running, anyway. The wellies they were wearing were fur-lined, and their feet must have been boiling in them. Fake-fur lining, but still. Closer to boating wear than combat boots, but ... not by much. Blue-grey camouflage pattern – they were cold weather gear. If there's one thing you can rely on in the military, absolute golden bloody rule in my experience, is cold weather gear arriving at the same time as the hot weather. Fake-fur-lined wellies worn with shorts, what a sight. Hairy legs, sunburn, fur-lined wellies! There was always the chance that they'd be embarrassed by their victory photos in time to come. Old and grey and red in the face, trying to impress their grandchildren. Trying to remember why it had seemed such a good idea to blast Uncle Barry into the lake, just because you moved your hand a few times and he didn't move his. Don't forget: *because he wasn't allowed to!* Same discipline both sides but I'm the one that comes a cropper. One in the eye for the uncle who isn't family, 'Colonel' who isn't even a soldier.

Micky took a big bite of his burger, and a lovely fat blob of ketchup got squeezed out from the halves of the bun, and fell guess where. Only onto one of his knees, just above the furry welly, at exactly the angle of incidence (I know this is technical) that made it slither down inside the lining of the boot before he had a chance to bend down and wipe it off. Magic!

Then he was looking over my shoulder, shading his eyes to see better. He can't have been the only one to notice something a bit out of the way, because next thing we knew someone was calling out 'Zombie alert!' There was a bit of a laugh in the voice, but not much of one. 'Zombies on the march!' Not exactly alarmed either. Note of caution, no more than that. Knowing we were in a country where surprises were never nice ones, and trained to see a bomb in every cigarette packet.

Group of people stumbling towards us. Every now and then one of them gave a wave, made a thumbs-up, maybe tried to smile. Their rate of progress was slow, but there was something relentless about it just the same. They weren't going to stop until they'd got where they meant to go. Maybe not until they got what they wanted.

Everyone laughed nervously when we heard the word 'zombie', and I'm not going to pretend I didn't join in. Still, it wasn't a serious warning or anything like. We could tell at a glance the figures stumbling towards us from the trees weren't zombies. Not the undead, not monsters hungry for a human snack. They were leftovers from a shitty sort of war, but something about the word wouldn't go away. It wasn't completely a joke. It seemed right, somehow, applied to these people who were alive but at the same time not quite. I'm not being nasty, but if bits of them had started dropping off, well ... it wouldn't have been a total shock. They'd had their lives taken away and not found a way back to them yet. Might not ever. Zombies was the wrong word but maybe – not being harsh, just looking facts in the face – maybe it was the right idea. Right general area. All in all, dead or undead, I couldn't say for sure. But one way or another, hungry. Sorely in need of a feed.

There were women in the shuffling group, but you couldn't tell right away. I'm not saying the chogie ladies looked like men, even if the lads often said so, it's just they were dirty and huddled together and the men shielded them a bit. Or maybe the men just moved faster and didn't care if the women got left behind. As they came towards us, the ranks moved to one side to let them through. I suppose it could have looked as if they were being invited to share our feast, sort of *Help yourself, plenty for everyone* message, if you didn't twig that the ranks were being a bit tactical. Defensive cordon round the beer. Can't guarantee the safety of all assets, so prioritize – doesn't need thinking about. Chances are the chogies didn't think about welcome or not welcome. They were guests at our barbecue the way we were guests in their country. Meaning they weren't guests at all, any more than we were. All of us gatecrashers pushing our luck. They could smell food and moved towards it. Hunger trance. Not something that needed thinking about either.

By most people's ideas there was plenty of chow on offer, but the ranks are big eaters, and there was just no knowing when the chogies would stop once they had started. There were burgers in buns and sausages in hot-dog rolls, those were the staples, laid out on paper plates. The chogies piled into those, no hesitation. Elbowing each other out of the way, getting stuck in. Mayonnaise and ketchup not required. They may not even have known condiments were there. I'm sure it's all right for Muslims to eat coleslaw, and as I say I've never liked the stuff – anyone can have my portion that wants it. But these chogies were hypnotized by meat aroma. Two of them grabbed a plate at the same time and tore it in two. A groan went up from the Saps, big hungry boys who can't bear to waste food, but they needn't have worried. The chogies pounced on what had been dropped, not bothering to wipe it before they went on wolfing it down.

Rodge grabbed hold of me, saying, 'Barry, we need to stop this! They shouldn't be eating the sausages!' What could I say? I agreed with him, but I didn't see what we could do about it. They were hungrier than we were, and they wouldn't take no for an answer. I didn't understand what he was on about. 'Where's your dictionary, Barry?' He wasn't making any sense, but I fetched the bloody dictionary anyway. I'd got into the habit of having it in my kit, though it had never been the slightest use. I'd point at a word to explain something to a chogie and get nowhere. Nowhere at all. Shrugs, shakes of the head.

The lads were drunk but not *drunk* drunk. Still in the driving seat, responsible for their actions. Toucan rule left behind but not too hard to catch sight of ... in the rear-view mirror. They could back up a bit and be sober. Ten minutes away from full control, half an hour at most.

Then Rodge was riffling frantically through the dictionary and saying, 'Here it is! We have to tell them the sausages are *derr*! Come on! *Derr*! *Derr*!'

I think it was *derr*, though languages and me ... I think I said. Rodge was deadly serious, whatever he was trying to get across, and after I started shouting '*derr*!' too, the lads joined in. Soon all of us were chorusing *derr* like a bunch of utter morons. Like something from Monty Python – The Peace-Keeping Forces and Attached Civilians Who Go *Derr*. But doing our best to pass on a message. Finally I had twigged.

We were telling them they were eating pork. Of course, with just the one word from the dictionary we couldn't make our meaning clear, couldn't say *the burgers are beef but the sausages are unclean*. '*Derr*!' was the best we could do. If I've even got the right word. If *derr* in Albanian really means pork. We only had the one word to pass on, but we gave it a lot of welly.

Whatever we said had an effect right away. There were little cries of horror, and one woman – now we could see there were women in the group – knelt down and threw up. Still ... before long she was back with her paper plate for a second helping, and this time she kept it down. I suppose ... what it comes down to. Starving Muslim still a Muslim, pork still pork. But food still food. I won't say there was a harmonious atmosphere at the barbecue, we weren't mingling or anything like, but if the chogies had just taken the cooked food that was laid out ready on the trestle table, and then pushed off, everything would have been okay. It needn't have been a big thing. At a picnic you get ants. At a barbecue, when it's a barbecue in a country that has been brought to its knees, you'll get starving gate-crashers – just one of those things.

Then one of the chogies, maybe the leader, if there was a leader, matted beard and staring eyes, made to grab a burger off the barbecue itself, meat that was still being cooked. Micky, caveman in charge, he didn't take kindly to that.

If Micky had been holding a spatula, if he was holding tongs, then he'd have waved those. Meaning *shoo!* and nothing more than that. Get on out of it. Push off. Territorial reflex. But that wasn't what he was holding. He was holding a flamethrower and so he waved that, with his finger on the trigger. Me, I've never held a flamethrower, don't know how one behaves, how the grip of it works at rest, all those tricky questions of balance and feel, but I know one thing from that afternoon at NRA Bisley. My Galil not the first or last tool to show a preference. Kit can surprise you. Kit can turn out to have a mind of its own.

I don't know what the flamethrower sounded like to the chogies, our guests who hadn't been invited. It made a noise that was a sort of hollow roaring, not nice. Stopped me in my tracks, I have to say. Didn't know what to think. Had some poor sod picked up a cigarette packet and been blown up?

Tongue of flame, that's what people always say. It's what you read in the papers, 'Tongue of Flame'. Can't quarrel with it. And if this tongue-of-flame was saying something, no arguments about what it was. *Get the fuck away from us, you animals.* Nothing about being guests in their country just for the minute.

Fight or flight, isn't it, when your body goes to action stations. It's instant. It charged me right up. You can't stand down at a moment's notice, just because you realize it was a false alarm. That's not how we're made.

With the chogies it was fight or flight, too, but it was always going to be flight. They'd seen too much in their time to stick around. They'd seen what happened to the ones who stood their ground and they went for the exit right away.

You'd have to have had a lot of experience having fire chucked at you to know, any one time, what was meant by it. We didn't have a translator with us, not expecting to come across chogies, live chogies. It would have to be quite a top-class translator to get the message across anyway. This particular tongue-of-flame of Micky's meant something like

Shit, that scared me.

Didn't mean to do that.

Burger grease on fingers, part of it.

Really sorry. Except ... quite a shock when all those chogies showed up. Still scared now, scared a fair bit.

Big ask even for a lingo merchant, champion interpreter, getting all that into sodding Albanian! Challenge even for the sort who orders food in restaurants anywhere in the world, has the locals going gaga over his accent and his vo-cab-u-lary.

Most of the chogies scattered right away. They sloped off. Shuffled, hobbled. But one stayed put – the one who'd reached for the meat on the barbecue, who kept on eating. Just kept on filling his face. Picked up paper plates from the ground where they'd been dropped when Micky pulled the trigger on the flamethrower. He didn't care about buns – just grabbed the meat from inside and stuffed it into his mouth. I couldn't tell whether he was looking past us or not seeing us at all. He coughed and spluttered as he chewed but managed to keep it down. The buns ended up on the ground.

The other chogies had rags wrapped round their feet, but this one had shoes, matching pair and everything. He was wearing red footie trainers, dirty and faded, nothing fancy – the sort of thing kids want at Christmas, and are the best thing ever, till getting towards Easter time. When I looked again, they were too small for him, not child-sized but maybe junior-sized. Shoes that someone had, that someone didn't need any more.

You have to be getting on a bit these days to remember when people didn't much care about gym shoes – daps we called them.

He'd opened up the front of the shoes to make room for his toes. I didn't notice at first because he was wearing brown socks, or maybe dirty bandages, could be crusted with old blood. Not a neat job opening up the shoes, not cut with a knife. Maybe just torn. My guess is, if these chogies had come across a knife in their travels there was a mean bastard on the other end of it. Not offering them the handle.

When there was nothing left to eat he looked down at his paper plate and then threw it away. It sailed towards us – like a frisbee, it flew just like a frisbee. Then it skittered off to the side at the last moment. As frisbees also do. I don't know if it was aimed at us. Perhaps it was. We all watched it land, and then he moved. Stumbled off after the rest. He moved more freely than the others, so perhaps it wasn't old blood after all, just brown socks. He was the only one of the bunch who looked as if he might have been able to fight if he had to, so maybe he was their protector. Maybe he needed to keep his strength up. Throwing away the buns – he was going all out for protein.

We felt a bit flat after the chogies had finally gone. Understatement! Even the Saps didn't feel so clever about winning the forfeit. The chogies had pissed on their parade. We were sorry for them, no question, but we were also pissed off with them for coming our way in the first place. We weren't just having a knees-up, whatever it looked like. We were there for a reason, and no-one was really having fun, just making the best of a bad job.

We did a bit of tidying, mainly to feel better. There's no washing up after a barbecue, that's the whole point. Rodge couldn't get over the sound of the flamethrower. He kept telling me what he made of it. *You know what it was like,* he said, *when Micky let loose? Angel of Death, that's what. Angel of Death blowing out all the fucking candles on my birthday cake.*

Toucan rule well behind him by that time. Beer making him think the deep thoughts again. Oirish thoughts. Or maybe there was something I was missing. Maybe it really was his birthday that day – actual birthday – and none of us had remembered. Now that I'm thinking of it, that would make a lot of sense.

If they'd known what the lads were facing the next day, I reckon even a bunch of starving chogies would have cut them some slack. I can imagine them saying, *Sorry mate, we weren't to know.* Or almost. Not smiles all round, obviously, but no lasting harm done. No new harm done. Hopefully.

It was the Saps had to stay in that little camp and start

on the dirty work next day. We got to go home to lovely welcoming BritFor Lines! I was looking forward to my nice modular bunk, space but not too much of it. Very quiet in the Land Rover. The plumb bob was an Evans, Welsh so born scowling, but you'd have to say none of us was happy. I don't know why plumb bobs are always Welsh. Tunnelling instinct, could be. Maybe it's the best you can do when the pits have closed. Get yourself below the surface, even if it's just a little bit.

Rodge asked, 'How long will it take?'

I couldn't tell him. Had to be a few days. Maybe a week. You need a baseline if you're not just making a guess, point of comparison, and we didn't have anything like that. Not the sort of thing you can look up in books!

We couldn't have explained to the chogies, any more than we could explain Micky didn't mean anything by the Tongue of Flame. More work for a translator! 'You know when the water supply came back to Pristina and at first everyone was happy – but then after a while people started complaining about the taste? Well, you know what you're like! You people haven't got a clue about rubbish disposal.' Not *you*, the people who gate-crashed our barbecue, just general *you*. Chogies as a group. National character. How people are, can't help themselves. No infrastructure, no waste collection, of course, all builds up, so what do you do with your rubbish? Cart it up to the mountains, dump it up there. And then, bit of rain, it all washes down again. Everyone in Pristina knee deep in all the assorted crap you thought you'd got rid of. And you're surprised to see it turn up again! *Every time.*

The water we drank looked like liquid shit when we pumped it up, I'm not joking, the muck that went into raw water storage, but once it had passed through absolute filters, 1-micron filter cartridges, it was nicer than what comes out of the taps in Southend. We always whacked in some bromine to play safe, though, in case some nasties had slipped through the single-micron net. Great stuff, bromine, and magic for healing small cuts and scrapes, not so quick in winter but just fantastic in the hot weather. We all swore by it. 'So we just thought you'd messed up the water supply with what we call *fly-tipping* back home ...'

Good luck translating 'fly-tipping' into Albanian! Nothing to do with flies, I don't think, though you never know.

'Golden rule of fly-tipping: dump it where it can't come back to you. Learn the drill and dump it downstream. Contaminated water supply – classic own goal. Lack of nous. So we didn't take the whole thing seriously. General idea – get back to us when you've mastered the principles of fly-tipping. It was weeks before we got round to testing the water, and then it turned out ... guess what? You were hundred per cent right ...'

Translators get to pass on some rotten shit, but everyone has their limits, don't they? Some things it's a case of better not to know. We didn't even talk about it that much. It wasn't like *Brookside*, body buried under the patio and the whole country talks of nothing else. One body! Much bigger scale, here. Industrial, you'd have to say.

Then it came to me. *Miss Adie!* Kate Adie would be able to find the words, tell the chogies what was going on, stop them thinking we were bastards who wouldn't share a barbecue. Wouldn't expect her to sugarcoat it, though.

Kate Adie holding her microphone, looking grim – don't suppose she's seen much to make her smile in her line of work – saying, 'Earlier today, civilian auxiliaries attached to the Royal Engineers as part of the NATO peacekeeping mission in Kosovo waited patiently to be rescued from the contaminated waters after their home-made craft capsized. They felt proper twerps, as who wouldn't.' She wouldn't bother with that, though, she go for something meatier. 'Refugees. Displaced persons. People who'd seen their country torn apart, hunger their only crime. Driven away from food with a tongue of flame ... by the very people who were supposed to bring back hope. To a country in despair.'

And that's us. Can't say it's a lie but it's not the whole truth. License payers, not to mention tax payers, don't they deserve to know everything? And the BBC has to give balance, has to. Fair's fair. She'd need to look at things from another angle. Clarification. New informa-tion. Come back to do an updation like the high-class journalist she is. She'll find the words. It's what she does.

I see her in a parka, the fur round her face, her hair whipping in the bitter wind, snowflakes landing on her eyelashes. 'Is there to be no end to the sufferings of this country? As if it wasn't enough to be terrorized and per-secuted ... then left to freeze and starve when the Serbians left. And now it seems that this deceptively beautiful landscape, tranquil nesting ground, I'm told, of the pygmy cormorant, conceals ... one more grisly secret.'

It looks as if she's trying not to cry – fighting back tears, as they say. It might be the wind in her face, or just the brightness of the lights. But of course it couldn't be like that. It wasn't the cold season by boat race time. It was the other one, other hell, hot one. Bit more pleasant in the evening. Windows wound down in the Land Rover. Driving on the right, out of politeness. Bit pissed but not bothered. Nobody to care. Not a breathalyser for hun-dreds of miles. Perhaps when we got nearer the city I'd be able to smell flowers.

'Tests on the water supply to the capital, Pristina,

showed that it was contaminated ... contaminated with human DNA. And there was only one likely place for the contamination to come from ...'

It didn't take any detective work, was it? Not little grey cells, not apply-my-method, not one-more-thing from bloody Lieutenant Columbo. There were bodies everywhere in that country. There were bodies hiding all over the place. No end to them. Whole hidden population. Hiding better than they had the last time someone came looking. We'd all seen them turn up, out of nowhere as often as not. We'd seen snowdrifts, snowdrifts that had turned to slush on the quiet, just give a lurch and belch out corpses. Waves of bodies sliding out onto the road. Why wouldn't there be bodies in any place you cared to mention? Any field, any ridge, any gully, any lake.

'Royal Engineers deployed as part of the NATO peace-keeping mission have the terrible task of retrieving bodies from the overflow funnel in Batlava Lake, the reservoir for Pristina – and Podujevo, if you're interested.'

Hundreds of them. Jam-packed inside the funnel.

'The BBC has been told that the Sappers, the Saps as they are known locally, will not be expected to identify the bodies of the ... chogies as they are known locally. That will be a matter for the War Crimes Commission, whatever that is and wherever based. Haven't a clue. The Saps will, however, have to reassemble the dead as best they can. After so long in the water the bodies are likely to be in an advanced state of...' She'd find a better word than fubar. Wouldn't say fubar, wouldn't say gunge. It's her job to keep things just that little bit vague, isn't it? She'll know how to say it so people watching at home don't throw up.

Then the sign-off that tells you it's all right to make a cup of tea, if you've even been watching in the first place. 'This is Kate Adie ...' catch in her throat, can't quite find the words, 'for BBC News and Barry Ashton, reporting from Batlava Lake.'

Fitzcarraldo Editions
8-12 Creekside
London, SE8 3DX
United Kingdom

ISBN 978-1-913097-62-2

Design by Ray O'Meara
Typeset in Fitzcarraldo
Printed and bound by TJ Books

fitzcarraldoeditions.com

Fitzcarraldo Editions